Echoes of a Silent Cradle

An Intricate Story of Love, Fate and Faith

Anilkumar P., Cherpu

BlueRose ONE.com
Stories Matter
NewDelhi • London

BLUE ROSE PUBLISHERS
India | U.K.

BlueRose ONE
Stories Matter
NewDelhi • London

For permissions requests or inquiries regarding this publication, please contact:

BLUE ROSE PUBLISHERS
www.BlueRoseONE.com
info@bluerosepublishers.com
+91 8882 898 898
+4407342408967

ISBN: 978-93-7310-201-6

Cover design: Daksh
Typesetting: Tanya Raj Upadhyay

First Edition: January 2026

In Memory of

Madhavi Amma – Great Grand Mother

K Raman Nair – Grand Father

Swaroop P Nair – Nephew

Bhagirathi Amma – Grand Mother

Nagath Narayanan Nair – Father

Kumaran P – Maternal Uncle

Deepak R – Childhood Friend

Dedicated to:

Suseela P.

Sajitha P.

Priya Muhammad Ali T. P.

Adv. Seema Menon

Latha Murali

Nanditha

Ajitha K.

Geetha Chirayath

Rathi S. Nair

Ranjana P.

Kamala K.

Sarojini Amma (Vavamma)

Lilly Athman

Ammini Chechi (Late)

Dhanya Shaju

Sunitha Murali

Prasanna P.

Rathi Devi

Jayasree

Sathi Devi

Kavitha Venugopal

Saritha Santhosh

Rajeswary U.

Hema K.

Merly P. C.

Rekha A.

Rekha Mohandas

Rama Devi K.

Sini & Mini

Noorjahan

Lalitha

Sobha I.

Maimunath

Special Dedication: To my beloved teachers, who have etched themselves, in my heart, I offer my deepest gratitude. You have imparted invaluable lessons on love, respect, pedagogy, and the virtues of simplicity and humility. Your unwavering support has been my guiding light, enabling me to navigate the complexities of this world. I salute each one of you, and my entire life shall be a prayer of thanksgiving for the profound impact you've had on my journey.

Acknowledgement

I am deeply grateful to Goddess Durga (Cherpu Bhagavathy) for blessing this endeavour with success. I would also like to express my heartfelt gratitude to Reshmi Reghunath for her invaluable support throughout this project.

From my childhood, my village has been a constant source of inspiration and strength for my writing. The events, festivals, and folklore of my hometown have greatly influenced me. My novel is centred entirely around the village of Cherpu (West) ~ Thrissur. Above all, I extend my sincere thanks to my mentors, friends, and well-wishers, whose words of encouragement and motivation have been a tremendous source of support.

I hereby pay a heartfelt and grand tribute to my dear friends—

Rajeesh T. R.

Gokul K. A.

Murali V.

Rajesh P.

Sijo Jose

Sudheeshkumar K. V.

V. G. Saji (Trivandrum)

Rahul K. A.

Raghul K. A.

M. Sujithkumar

Shaju Paruvath

Shiju Paruvath

Rajeesh T. (Trivandrum)

Sreedhar Balakrishnan Swamy

Pramod P. R.

Mohandas – Uncle

Naveen Mohan

Sabarish

Rajeev Menon

and Swarag P Nair — my nephew ~ for their unwavering support and encouragement in helping me achieve this goal.

I extend my deepest gratitude to the esteemed writer, Gopikrishnan Kottoor, whose meticulous review and insightful corrections have been instrumental in shaping my novel. His expert guidance has not only refined the structure and language of the book but has also enriched its very essence. I am indebted to him for his unwavering support and invaluable counsel, without which this book would not have attained its present form. His contribution to my work is a testament to the power of collaboration and generosity of spirit that defines the literary community.

Foreword

'Echoes of a Silent Cradle' is a well narrated story that has interesting and varied layers that add to the story's subtleties. The story is interesting for its depiction of unconventional themes of gender equality, and of twists of love and life's ardours set against an orthodox and conventional backdrop. There are visual qualities in the narration that attract and sustain the reader's interest. Human relationships that seem to appear by chance, are controlled by an unknown destiny. The references to the Hindu Gods, the philosophies of religious justice, and of fate of the characters written in the stars are well-etched.

The characters put on flesh and blood and are easily recognizable and identifiable as people living amongst us.

Reading "Echoes of a Silent Cradle" has been an absorbing, appealing, and touching experience for the journeys and illuminating adventures that the book offers.

■ *Gopikrishnan Kottoor*

Prologue

When the announcement echoed through the auditorium, a thunderous applause erupted ~ like a hailstorm of joy. Then came the words: "Raghav Nair" and the title of my fiction, *The Soulmates*. I rose slowly and walked toward the dais.

I wore a golden-coloured *kasavu* dhoti and a white linen shirt, a gift from my maternal uncle. It was the same attire I usually wore to the temple—simple, traditional, and deeply personal. That's the dress code I cherished the most.

I mounted the stage, went near the chief guest, who was entrusted with presenting the awards. From his hands, I received a large cheque and a gleaning memento. I bowed and touched his feet with reverence, offering a silent tribute. It was the first time in my life I had been publicly recognized—for a novel that was uniquely mine.

With quiet pride swelling inside me, I returned to my seat. Adhiti sat beside me, her smile radiant and her eyes wide with astonishment. As I settled in, she gently patted my shoulder.

"You did it well. I'm proud of you—and fond of you."

That moment marked the beginning of a new chapter in my life. I had waited so long for this: a moment of joy, of fulfilment, of quiet triumph. My eyes welled up. Tears rolled down my cheeks. Adhiti watched silently, then wiped them away with her handkerchief. I removed my spectacles and wiped my eyes once again.

I handed the awards to Adhiti—my legacy. Sometimes, daughters are a father's greatest pride. Each daughter is a princess in her father's eyes, isn't she? Adhiti may not be my daughter by blood, but by *karma*, she is mine. She is my legacy.

After the ceremony, we returned to Rajeesh's home in Thiruvananthapuram—the sacred city where Lord Vishnu rests his head upon the hood of the mighty serpent *Anantha*. The house itself was unique, with a canopy that hooded the upper reaches through which sunlight seeped in. My friend Rajeesh, a courteous fellow who treats everyone with warmth and generosity was delighted to see me.

He ordered dinner from outside. Since my daughter is a passionate foodie, he arranged non-vegetarian food ~ Schezwan Fried Rice with Pepper Chicken. Being a vegetarian since childhood, I just had some salads and chapatis. His daughter and Adhiti are about the same age and get along well together.

The next day, after visiting *Lord Padmanabha*, I went to Rajeesh's house for breakfast. They served *idlis* with sambar made with ground coconut. It was delicious, and I've loved this preparation since my boyhood. As I ate, I suddenly remembered my *Ammumma's* face. She was an expert at making *varutharacha sambar*.

After breakfast, I was told that I had a guest coming to interview me. I was surprised – it was my first experience like this. Adhiti had already gone to a movie with Priya. I stepped out onto the porch and saw a lady dressed like a reporter. She had a tag around her neck announcing that she was a media person. She introduced herself as Hiba Fathima, along with the name of her news channel.

At first, I told her I wasn't in the mood to talk. But when she insisted and reminded me that I was her teacher in the higher secondary, I agreed.

She said, "Sir, you were my English teacher in Higher Secondary."

"I can't quite remember, my child," I replied hesitantly.

She quickly took a watch from her bag and asked, "Do you remember this?"

It was an old, worn-out watch. I asked, "What's this?"

She smiled and said, "This is the watch you gave me for my achievement in the terminal examinations. I scored full for English."

I was shocked and said, "Now I remember! You're one of the students from Palakkad, right? Yes, I remember. After the higher secondary, your parents were so adamant when you wanted to do higher studies, right? I met them and asked your *vappachi* to send you to college. "Hey Hiba, it's so good to see you after such a long time – twenty years! And now you're a reporter? That's wonderful! A reporter for a reputed channel... I'm really proud of you, dear. So, what else?" I asked.

She hesitated and then said, "Sir, I need to interview you. I know you might not be ready for it, but I badly need it for my promotion."

I smiled and replied, "Since this is for you, I have no objection, dear."

Then she asked, "Are you still single?"

I just nodded a "Yes."

"Sorry, sir," she quickly apologized.

"It's... it's okay," I said, a little awkwardly.

She continued, "Sir, in your novel, on the dedication page, there's a sentence. It goes like this," and she read it aloud:

"Dedicated to my mother and my intimate, sincere and smart friends whose lives shaped my career and had a far-reaching impact on me."

Hiba looked at me curiously and asked, "Raghav sir, who are they?"

I smiled and said, "Yes... let me start from the beginning..."

While we talked, she put her mobile phone on recording mode. I continued, "There are two of them – Madhav, and Ganesh.

I was born in the southern part of Karnataka – the land of folklore and the village of Gulbarga. It's a place full of superstition, *Yakshagana*, and simple country folk with very straightforward manners. After my mother's death, my childhood unfolded in Thrissur, where I was brought up in the quiet shadow of her absence. Thrissur is the land of *poorams* and cultural events. But even then, I didn't find much comfort. My surrogate mother and grandmother became my strength and spiritual guides. The village has always been my passion and the source of energy behind everything I do academically. Even though I wasn't her biological son, I always felt a strong bond with my *Amma* and *Ammumma*. *Amma* is Radhasree, and *Ammumma* is Bhagirathi."

Table of Contents

Saga of Madhav

From the first standard onwards, Madhav and I were friends. As far as I am concerned, he is my soulmate. The term "friend" in Sanskrit is *thozhan*, which signifies a companion close to one's heart.

My first standard class teacher was Rugmani. The name Rugmani is familiar from the *Mahabharata*, as it belongs to the first wife of *Lord Krishna*, an incarnation of Vishnu in human form. Rugmani teacher was a graceful and kind educator. At times, I would associate her with my mother, though my mother is even more beautiful. She has a fair complexion.

The school was a Lower Primary School located in Thrissur. The buildings had tiled roofs and were scattered across the campus. In the month of *Karkkidakam* (mid-July), I became acquainted with Madhav for the first time. His facial features reminded me of the idol of *Lord Krishna* at *Guruvayur*. He had a pleasant personality and was always smiling. From that day onward, I made it a habit to sit beside him on the front bench.

During those days, we did not bring lunch from home. Both of us would return home during the lunch hour.

Lunch hours typically extended from 1:00 pm to 2:00 pm, except on Fridays, when lunch was from 12:30 pm to 2:00 pm to allow Muslim students to attend Jummah prayers at the mosque. Fridays were especially enjoyable for us, as the longer lunch break gave us ample time to explore nearby fields, orchards, and ponds.

Fridays are considered auspicious and are dedicated to the worship of the goddess Durga or Lakshmi ~ the deities of wealth, wisdom and prosperity. After studying my horoscope, an albino soothsayer noted that I have the Moon in the fifth house, indicating that I am a devotee of the Goddess. The Moon, being the most beautiful satellite in the zodiac, is associated with mental states, as it is prone to waxing and waning. The fifth house is said to represent the mind, previous birth, and children. So, I haven't a stable mind at all. My mind is always wavering. I couldn't make a firm decision. *Ammumma* was well versed in astrology and occult studies. But my date of birth is not known to her exactly. That's why the prophecy of that albino soothsayer is the only version to stick on my future.

Even when Rugmani teacher asked questions, I often struggled to answer on the first attempt and required extra time. Unlike Madhav, I was not particularly clever. Madhav was popular among both boys and girls in the class, admired for his elegant attire and cheerful demeanour. Yet, he felt most comfortable in my company.

He would wear white sandal paste (*chandana*) on his forehead, while I adorned mine with turmeric paste, which is yellow in colour and associated with the goddess. Madhav aspired to become an architect. I often noticed him collecting pictures of buildings in an old notebook, eventually gathering over two hundred images.

In the second standard, Parukutty was our class teacher. Unlike Rugmani, she was of moderate height and darker complexion, short and husky in build. She retired midway through the year and was replaced by Sajitha, a Muslim teacher who always wore a scarf and no bindi, whereas the previous teachers had worn bindis between their eyebrows.

In the second standard, Madhav and I became even closer. We would sometimes go to Madhav's house for lunch, and at other times he would accompany me home. Being a Brahmin, Madhav was a strict vegetarian. His favourite dishes were *masala dosa* and *curd rice*, while I preferred *sadhya* with *payasam*. I loved the food prepared by *Ammumma* more than that of my mother, though I cared for both.

In 1988, we moved on to the third standard under the guidance of Paapathi teacher. She was plump and styled her hair artificially in a graceful manner. Her complexion was neither very fair nor dark, and she wore a diamond nose ring. Her voice was powerful, and I particularly enjoyed her Malayalam lessons. She had a special fondness for both Madhav and me. Her earrings were made of beads, and the bindi on her forehead was as large as that of Paro in the film *Devadas*. She applied a generous amount of *kumkum* to her hair. That year, both Madhav and I suffered from chickenpox, a frightening illness at the time. We contracted it around the same period and were quarantined for three weeks. *Ammumma* explained that it was a curse of Goddess *Kali* – a "dance of destruction."

In the fourth standard, we had Saraswathi teacher, named after the goddess of learning. This was the year we began studying English as a second language. I started learning the English alphabet in March 1989, treating both lowercase and uppercase letters with equal importance. Saraswathi's Mathematics lessons were unique. She was also the one to slap me with a stick for the first time during this year, but I appreciated her teaching methods and class. Her hair was long, and her eyes large; at times, she would glare at us, which made the students nervous. Madhav and I frequently talked about various topics, sometimes even supernatural elements like sylphs and gnomes. His storytelling about *Kaali Paru*, an oral tale passed down from our ancestors, was fascinating. According to the story, *Kaali Paru*, an outcaste woman, committed suicide by jumping into a pond. Since then, the area was believed to be haunted by her ghost, which would attack women who went there before sunrise to bathe – a common practice at the time.

In 1990, we entered the fifth standard, our last year at that primary school. Indira teacher was our class in-charge. She was an excellent teacher, and her voice still echoes in my memory. She often compared our friendship to that of Krishna and Arjuna, asking, "Are both of you here today?" Her smile was unique, and I enjoyed her English lessons, particularly her clear pronunciation and teaching methods.

She taught "This" and "That" along with "These and Those" in a way that made learning easy. She also introduced us to the rhyme "Jack and Jill went up the hill," though Madhav preferred "This is the house that Jack built," which he often sang during lunch breaks.

In the sixth standard, we joined a new Government school located about two kilometres from our old school. We began bringing lunch from home regularly. That year, the school achieved a 100% result in the 10th standard for the first time in Kerala among government schools. Jameela teacher, a strict disciplinarian, taught English and mathematics. The first chapter of our English textbook, *The Bangle Seller*, still stays with me. It narrates the story of a bangle seller who steals a rich child's doll, only for his daughter to later return it.

The second chapter, "Hobbies," included a glossary explaining that hobbies are leisure-time activities and not professions. I once asked Madhav, "What's this hobby business?" He replied, "Hobbies are things we do in our free time. We can start collecting stamps from today onwards!"

In 1991, we entered the seventh standard with Malathy teacher handling Malayalam. She recited poems beautifully and explained them with care. Her hair often covered her ears, and she wore large black-framed spectacles. That year, Janaki teacher also taught English. Her class was excellent, and she introduced us to the poem *Night* by William Blake, teaching us to appreciate nighttime as a period of peace and wonder. I began observing the night differently after her lessons.

In the eighth standard, the school became overcrowded due to its outstanding results. We were split into different batches. I was placed in the E division and Madhav in the A division. However, my mother insisted that I be admitted to the same batch as Madhav, and the teacher, though reluctant, agreed. Usha was our class teacher. I still remember her face clearly. Her first English lesson, *A Passage to India*, covered various Portuguese and British expeditions to India. We studied and even napped together. We also attended poorams, films, and dramas together.

I first witnessed the Thrissur *Pooram* festival with Madhav. His father took me along that day. The festival is renowned for its spectacular display of sixty caparisoned elephants, vibrant percussion ensembles like *Pandimelam* and *Panchavadyam,* and a grand finale of fireworks. An additional ceremony called *Kudamattom* is held in the afternoon, while *Ilanjithara Melam* is the main highlight of the festival. Celebrated in the month of *Medam* (April or May), we stayed awake the entire night watching the fireworks. It was a thrilling and unforgettable experience.

In 1993, when we entered the ninth standard, our bond grew even stronger. Madhav had a keen interest in general knowledge and current affairs, which I rarely paid attention to. I, on the other hand, was passionate about English and Malayalam. Since childhood, I had loved stories, fairy tales, and supernatural accounts passed down by my great-grandmother, Madhavi *Amma*. Madhav, however, was more pragmatic in his approach. Our class teacher, Ramani, taught Hindi, the national language of India and one of the widely spoken languages across India.

Her lessons on *Meera Bhai* and *Baba Amte* still echo in my mind. Her method of teaching was unlike any other—gentle, thoughtful, and deeply engaging. That year, we also became acquainted with two new teachers: Vijaya Lakshmi, who taught English, and Radha, who handled Mathematics. Vijaya Lakshmi's lecture on the poem *Sands of Dee* by Charles Kingsley left a profound impression on both Madhav and me. In those days, memorising poems was a requirement. However, after a new educational reform in Kerala post-2000, this practice was removed, and poems were asked only in comprehension questions during exams.

Yet, this particular poem touched our hearts, especially the concluding lines:

"But still the boatmen hear her call the cattle home Across the sands of Dee."

The poem narrates the tragic tale of Mary, a young girl who drowns in the Dee estuary while trying to gather her cattle before the rains arrive. Written in a melancholic tone, it depicts Mary's untimely death and the inevitability of fate. Though its message was sombre and pessimistic, we cherished it deeply.

In the tenth standard, Raman Mash became our class teacher. He was a strict disciplinarian, handling both English and Biology, and all the students feared him. Madhav and I received more than a few scoldings and even slaps from him for being talkative. He would deliberately switch our seats to keep us apart. Normally, we sat on the front bench–Madhav in the first seat, I in the second, followed by Praveen, Rajeesh, Gokul, Benoy, Shakeer, Apindas, Sujith and others.

The tenth standard was a whirlwind of anxiety and excitement. We were all eager to pass the SSLC exams and unsure about what lay ahead. There was an unspoken dread that we might be scattered, separated, and lost to each other. On the girls' side, Saritha Aratupuzha was our closest friend, though most of them were reserved in those days.

In the tenth standard, I especially enjoyed the second paper in Malayalam, *Dharmaraja* by C. V. Raman Pillai, a historical novel set in Travancore, and the second paper in English, *English in Indulekha*, which examined the influence of English education during Kerala's feudal era. The former delved into themes of social conflict and political struggle, while the latter critiqued caste divisions, child marriage, and superstition.

As per Hindu mythology, *Dharmaraja–Yama*, the god of death and justice–takes form as *Yudhishtira*, the eldest *Pandava*, known for his righteousness. Similarly, *Maharajah Karthika Thirunal Rama Varma* of Travancore, called *Dharma Raja*, ruled from 1758 to 1798 with strict adherence to *Dharma Sastra*. The novel explored themes of inheritance, politics, and societal values.

Indulekha traced the promotion of English education and the shifting landscape of nineteenth-century Kerala society.

It was a year of autographs, heartbreaks, career choices, and farewells. We knew that after this, we would rarely meet in such a carefree way again. One day, Madhav turned to me and said:

"You're lucky to have friends like them."

"And you're lucky too," I replied.

"One day this will all end," he said bleakly. "We'll all go our separate ways. No more silly pranks, chatting, love talks..."

"What's wrong with you, man? Wow... so philosophical. I've never heard anything like this," I teased.

"No way, dear," he replied.

"But we can always stay in touch," I said.

"That never happens, da... Life gets busy. Jobs, houses, money... Who knows what's in store for us!" His eyes clouded with worry.

He nodded, touched my cheek gently, and whispered, "Don't worry, my child. You'll always be my *thozhan*." He winked with his left eye and smiled–a smile so beautiful, so, heartfelt; it's etched in my memory forever.

After the SSLC exams, we were scattered. There were no mobile phones, no social media–just letters. Many homes didn't even have telephone connections. Only Madhav's house had a BSNL phone. The much-awaited SSLC results came in May. All students passed except one. Madhav, Rajesh, and Gokul scored above eighty percentage, while I scored sixty-seven percent. I wasn't disappointed–I had expected it. I struggled with Mathematics and Physics, but from the eighth standard onwards, I loved Malayalam and English more than any other subjects.

We memorised poems and lessons half-heartedly at times but managed to pass the exams with a sigh of relief. Madhav had a clear plan–he chose the second group, while I wavered without a definite goal. It was he who guided me.

"Raghav, you scored well in Social Science. Why not choose the third group as your specialisation?" he suggested.

I agreed and applied to Christ College, while he opted for St. Thomas College and was selected. I was waitlisted at rank 137.

Thus, we parted ways–a breakup not just of friendships but of shared lives. Breakups aren't limited to romantic relationships; they happen between friends too. Madhav settled in town with his uncle, while I stayed at my ancestral home. Though we kept in touch through letters–each inland letter costing only one rupee then–the distance between us widened.

Those days are gone. Today's instant communication can't replace the warmth of handwritten letters.

College Life

Pre-degree was my first real experience of campus life. From elections to seminars, cultural festivals, Onam celebrations, and Christmas events, every moment was golden. I studied diligently, and Madhav introduced me to competitive exams like the PSC and UPSC. Desperate for a job, I became obsessed with my studies.

In the first year, our class teacher was Stephen Sir, who taught Economics, and in the second year, it was Chandran Sir, who taught History. These years deepened my understanding of English literature, and I finally chose it as my major for my BA. The novel *Treasure Island* by Robert Louis Stevenson opened the world of adventure and imagination to me.

This was the novel that first introduced me to pirates and their escapades. Sasidharan Sir narrated it so vividly that I felt as though I was sailing alongside Jim, the protagonist. The descriptions of ships, sea breezes, and pirate life brought the story alive. I still recall the pirates' chant as the ship set sail:

"Fifteen men on the dead man's chest Yo ho ho and a bottle of rum."

The story, filled with treasure hunts and greed, also introduced me to French and Latin words. I first learned the term "marooned," meaning to be stranded without escape.

In the late 1990s, I even dreamt of the villain from the story. He was a fearsome figure with one leg.

I scored 98 out of 100 in English in the second-year exam. One of the questions asked us to describe the life of a captain at the Admiral Benbow Inn, and I answered with confidence.

Throughout those years, I collected inland letters from Madhav, each preserved in my library. Among them, one letter still haunts me:

Dear Raghav,

Hope you are well, under the grace of Goddess Durga. I received your letter yesterday and wrote back that very day.

How are your studies? I hope Economics and History haven't swallowed you whole! How are your new friends? Convey my regards to all.

I hope your Ammumma and Amma are doing well. I hope Ammumma's rheumatic pain has eased. Please send my regards.

You told me to write in detail so you can read it in the library for a long time–that's why I wrote this cover letter with care.

Today is Karkkidakam (last month of Malayalam calendar) *1st - my birthday month! You know my star is Vishakam in Karkkidakam. Last year, we visited Naalambala temples -*

Triprayar, Koodalmanikyam, Moozhikkulam, and Payammal - remember?

I miss you dearly, Raghav.

I am not fine at all, dear. My mind is turbulent–I don't know how to ease it. I couldn't tell you this face to face.

I pray that in the next birth; we will be born from your mother's womb together.

Goodbye, dear.

Yours,
Madhav

That was the last letter I ever received from him. I replied the next day, but no further letters came. I was anxious, troubled, and confused.

Two weeks later, I visited his college with Unni Warrier, a temple employee. Madhav hadn't been attending classes for weeks. His classmates didn't know anything. I went to his home in town to find that - it was locked. A reluctant neighbour eventually told me:

"Who are you to Madhav?"

"We've been childhood friends. I haven't seen him in a long time," I said eagerly.

"Please, tell me whatever you know. I request you," I added.

He hesitated and finally said, "I am Saji Bal, a police constable at East Station, Thrissur. Your friend is in a coma now."

"Coma?" I stammered, as if struck by lightning.

"Sir, I don't understand," I whispered.

"Coma is a state of paralysis caused by an attack or accident. Your friend was brutally attacked and hospitalised. His condition is rather critical," he explained.

My throat went dry, words deserted me, and I stood frozen.

"What... happened? How did this... happen?" I asked, desperate for answers.

"We don't know, dear boy. You had better go and see for yourself," he advised. "He's in RCC Hospital, Trivandrum now. Go, but first inform your family."

I returned home shattered. My chest felt heavy. On the bus, I sobbed uncontrollably. Unni Warrier consoled me, saying, "You must go, but I can't accompany you. Uma is alone at home. You should ask Sudheesh to go with you."

For the first time in my life, I felt the emptiness of not having a father by my side. I longed for his presence as I prepared to visit Trivandrum to see my friend.

The next day, Sudheesh and I set out. The journey was exhausting–we had no reservation and travelled in a crowded general compartment. But Sudheesh stayed by me, offering comfort throughout the ride. It took six hours to reach the capital city, the abode of Lord Vishnu. It was my first visit there, and truth be told, I hated it—it reminded me of Madhav's fate.

Would I ever meet Lord Vishnu? I wondered bitterly. I wanted to ask Him, "Why punish my friend like this? Why?"

My eyes filled with tears again and again; I could hardly see through the haze of grief.

The hospital was vast, and we struggled to find the correct ward. Fortunately, we met Madhav's father at the pharmacy. I clasped his hands and wept. He wiped my tears and led us to the ICU, but we were not permitted inside. Only Madhav's mother was allowed.

We waited. Waiting became the only task. Hopes, dreams, aspirations... all seemed suspended. We didn't know what the present was, let alone the future. There was nothing to do but sit, anxious and bored, without food or water. I couldn't eat. All I longed for was to see my friend's face, to speak with him, to feel his presence once more.

Sudheesh sat beside me silently.

Madhav's father confided that they too knew nothing of his condition.

"Why would he hide it?" he sobbed. "What's the issue? How did this happen?"

"He joined an entrance coaching centre in Cochin to prepare for engineering exams," his father explained. "A month ago, he told me he wanted to stay for group study—I agreed. But then I received a call... they said he had been ragged badly and was in critical condition. Nothing more..."

His voice broke. "I never knew... how much pain he must have endured..."

The last letter had been a month ago.

Just then, a siren wailed. A red light blinked on the ICU signboard as doctors and nurses hurried inside. We panicked and rushed after them, only to be stopped.

Moments later, Madhav's mother burst out, wailing and collapsing against her husband's chest.

"He... is... gone... gone..." she cried.

That moment shattered me. From then on, a void engulfed my life. I became alone—not just physically, but in spirit.

We never knew why it happened. His parents, friends: none of us knew. Yet, there had to be a reason, even if we couldn't grasp it.

Sometimes it is said that truth is stranger than fiction, as Jawaharlal Nehru wrote in *Discovery of India*: *"What is truth? I do not know for certain, and perhaps our truths are relative and the absolute truth is beyond us."*

It took years to erase those childhood memories, but Madhav's image lingered in my heart. Without him, I was hollow. He had been my guide, my confidant. I couldn't simply forget him: It wasn't easy at all.

I missed him with every breath I took, every minute of the day ~ while studying, meditating, praying. Sometimes, as I gazed at the idol of Goddess Durga, tears would blur my sight, and I would close my eyes for a long while.

I resolved to "hold on," but sometimes my strength faltered.

Ammumma comforted me. "If you feel this much sorrow, what of the sorrow of that poor bereaved mother, Madhav's mother? *Krishna... Krishnaa...* May her grief be eased. May that child's soul be liberated."

She then asked, "Raghava... do you believe in fate?"

"I don't know, *Ammumma*," I replied.

"Your grandfather always said fate governs everything. Even our intelligence follows fate. *Karma*, destiny–whatever you call it..."

"Whatever the reason, isn't this the worst sorrow a mother can face?" I cried. "Why did God punish them so cruelly? I've lost faith in Him!"

She gently asked, "What, according to you, is the greatest sorrow in life?"

"The loss of a son," I whispered.

"No, dear," she corrected. "Poverty is the greatest sorrow."

"I'm not arguing, *Amma*," I protested, "but will you tell me why poverty is worse?"

She smiled softly. "I'll tell you a story... one that teaches the weight of hunger and poverty."

And so, she narrated a tale from the mythology of *Lord Shiva* and *Goddess Parvathy*.

The Story of the Widow

Once, in a village, lived a poor widow with eight sons. They shared a deep bond, their love and wisdom drawn from their mother's guidance.

One day, joining the king's cavalry with the court clown, the brothers fought a battle against a neighbouring kingdom. All eight were killed, and their corpses were carried one by one to their mother's yard.

The bereaved mother sat beside them for days without food or water, crying endlessly. She wouldn't allow anyone to cremate the bodies, even as decay set in and the stench spread.

By the tenth day, hunger gnawed at her. Madness overtook her, and she hallucinated, craving food but unable to ask for help.

Shiva and *Parvathy*, disguised as travellers, witnessed her agony. *Parvathy* wept, saying, "Why this cruel fate? The grief of losing sons is unbearable... me lord"

Shiva replied, "No, *Devi*. Hunger is the worst sorrow. Let me show you."

He magically suspended a bunch of bananas above her reach. Desperate, she stacked her sons' corpses, one atop the other, and finally snatched the bananas, which she devoured without even peeling them.

"Now you understand," *Shiva* told *Parvathy*. "Hunger is the deepest pain."

Turning to me, *Ammumma* said, "Raghav, this may not be the perfect answer, but it helps us see that poverty and hunger are greater sorrows than any other."

Her story gave me no relief, but it deepened my understanding of fate's role in life. Before this, I had thought Madhav's mother's grief was the ultimate sorrow. After hearing the tale, I learned to bear my own anguish.

Healing, I realised, means breaking the cycle of negative thoughts and emotions that hold us captive. Losing someone dear is a wound that never fully heals, but accepting the loss is the first step toward moving forward. Grief remains with us until our final breath.

"Madhav... you left me all alone. Without you, I am lost. The care, the friendship you gave me wasn't enough. I crave it still. Perhaps we'll meet in another life. You mischievous *Kanaya*, butter thief, sly rogue... you abandoned me on this earth. I won't talk to you until we meet again."

Even after all these years, Madhav's face has never left me. There is no day in my life that does not carry the weight of his memory.

Saga of Ganesh

The name *Ganesh* itself evokes a powerful image: Lord Ganesha, the remover of obstacles. He is the son of Parvathy, the consort of Lord Shiva–the great ascetic and the master of *thandava*, the cosmic dance of destruction and renewal.

His form is strikingly unique: a human body with the head of an elephant, symbolising wisdom, strength, and compassion. His birth, too, is unlike that of any other divine being. According to Hindu mythology, Ganesha was created solely by Parvathy. She sculpted him from a paste of turmeric and breathed life into him. Once brought to life, she instructed him to stand guard at the entrance of her bath and not to let anyone pass.

Unaware of these events, Lord Shiva returned from his meditation and was stopped by this unfamiliar child. Enraged, Shiva severed Ganesha's head in fury. Heartbroken, Parvathy wept in despair, and Shiva, realising his grave mistake, replaced the lost head with that of an elephant. From that day onward, Ganesha became the one who must be worshipped first, before any other ritual or undertaking.

For me, the absence of Madhav has been an unbearable void for many years. I could never forget his smiling face or the warmth of our friendship. When Ganesh entered my life in my thirties, a strange comfort washed over me. His gestures, his expressions, his smile resembled Madhav's so closely that, at times, it felt as though fate had returned him to me. I fondly called him my second Madhav, sharing with him every memory and story of my friendship with the first.

There were moments when grief overtook me and I broke down in front of him, overwhelmed by the pain of losing Madhav. Ganesh, with quiet sympathy, would sit beside me, offering comfort without judgment.

Our friendship deepened during the years we worked together at a publishing firm in Bangalore. The city ~ alive with fashion, lights, and restless energy ~ was an exciting place to live, a melting pot of dreams and struggles. Ganesh's own life was marked by separation. His parents had parted ways when he was very young. He lived with his mother, Gouri, while his father remarried and settled in Canada. Such arrangements, though painful, are becoming increasingly common in contemporary society. I often reflect that, in the future, India may embrace the culture of single-parent families, much like the Western world already has done.

Despite all the complexities, our bond grew stronger. For both of us, friendship became a refuge—a space where shared laughter, tears, and memories could heal the wounds of the past.

"Sometimes that type of living with children is good for a woman, dear child. At least he left this son for me. That's the great relief," Gouri *Amma* said.

"In moments of reflection, I've come to realize that it's the children who give a woman's life its true meaning. And I'm grateful that he left me with this son; it's a solace, a reminder that not all is lost". Gouri *Amma* again told me.

She treated me as her own son. She didn't show any discrimination. She used to call me "Ram". I liked her cooking very much. I missed the flavours of *Ammumma's* cooking - when I left Thrissur. But I could feel *Ammumma* in Ganesh's mother and her food. Like me, Ganesh is also a vegan. He used to recite *Lalitha Sahasra Nama* in the early morning.

"This *mantra* is very powerful Raghav". This should be recited during *brahmamuhurtha*, i.e between 3:00 to 5:30 am" he said.

Later, he taught me how to recite it. The entire 180 verses are meant for chanting. It describes the Mother Goddess in various forms. The former part focuses on, Her appearance, while and the latter part highlights Her triumph of good over evil.

Gouri Amma belonged to a great family and carried a name with respect. She owned a huge mansion in the heart of Bangalore.

"Ram, take care of my son at the office because he is very straight forward and says everything plainly. Some people don't like that" she often said.

"Yes *Amma*, I will" I replied.

"He turned 31 this month of *Makaram* (January). I want to arrange his marriage as early as possible. Only then will he become calmer. His anger will lessen, right?" She said.

"Yes, it's a good idea" I nodded.

"Ram, you better ask him about it. When I brought up marriage, he became enraged."

"*Amma*, don't worry. I will talk to him "I said.

" Ram, you are the same age as Ganesh. Are you looking for a marriage? "Gouri *Amma* asked.

"No, not yet. I am badly in need of a Government job *Amma*. I used to write some PSC tests. My *Amma* used to tell me that a Government service is essential for us. "I told her.

"I know marriage is a horrible adjustment. He knows everything about my life. But whenever he needs a partner... I want to die peacefully after that" Gouri *Amma* sighed.

I was looking at her face and sighed too.

"Have you read the book *Agnisakshi* by *Lalithambika Antharjanam*? It's a Malayalam novel," Gouri *Amma* said.

"No, not yet. But *Amma* told me about that book once. It's an encyclopaedia of human relationships" I replied.

"That novel influenced me a lot dear, especially in the postmarital period" she said.

"What is the main theme of that novel?" I asked.

"It tells the story of a Nambudiri woman named Devaki, who is drawn into the struggle for social and political emancipation but cannot easily shake off the chains of customs that bind her. Devaki struggled a lot and finally she became a *yogini*. "Gouri *Amma* continued.

"In the novel there is a dialogue of Thankam's mother, that is very true even in this century. Life as a woman is horrible.... Even if you're born as a dog for ten births, it's okay... but one should not be born as a Brahmin woman.", she sighed again.

"That's the pathetic state of a woman. It cannot be changed, dear. Society is still male-dominated. Even though in the 21st century, the situation is improving, gender bias still exists," Gouri *Amma* murmured.

"I struggled a lot at the hands of Ganesh's father, you know.... It was a period of crisis, Ram. He became wild sometimes. Living with a drunkard is easy, living with a robber is easy ~ but living with a man who is jealous and emotionally complex is a Herculean task. My life became more horrible than ever. It was a bed of woes. I had a job when I got married. This man tried his best to kick me out of my job. But fate had other plans. He couldn't do it, despite his influence. My father helped me throughout. He was a learned advocate in the High Court. So, I escaped. According to me, all children (girls) should be educated. Every woman needs a job ~ It is mandatory. But our society didn't believe that. They are always in search of a partner for each girl. That might be a stranger. We don't get to know that stranger easily. Estrangement and mutual bickering are part of marital life. But if this relationship contains even a little bit of LOVE, then it becomes beautiful. When LOVE is absent, there will be doubts. I survived that marital disharmony with the help of that Government job. I was a teacher by profession – High School Assistant in English. You are in search of a teacher's job, right? That's why I thought I have a connection with you, because all teachers' minds are sometimes alike. During my college days, I was proposed to by many men. But in those days, it was a forbidden fruit like in *Paradise Lost Book IX*. Now I regret it. The only achievement of this disharmony is Ganesh. God has given me a good son. When I saw Ganesh's face, I gradually forgot the cruelties of that man. May be that's what is called LIFE. Ganesh has big dreams and aspirations. He wants to settle in Western countries, especially the Netherlands and the UK. I don't know what is special about those places. He always tells me that this place is not good for growth and potential. He says he is creative. How can I go with him? You should better speak to him, right? It's my great ambition that Ganesh should be married to a good girl ~ not by appearance but by character. I am okay with a poor village girl. You'd better ask him, right? Whenever I talk about marriage, he becomes wild like his father. Is there a girl in his life? What are you people talking about? Any love-talk? Any girlfriend? If he has any girlfriend, I am okay with that. Please tell him, Ram," Gouri *Amma* finally stopped her long talk. It felt like a monologue – her long struggle with marital disharmony.

"I will enquire *Amma*.... Sure ...... next time," I answered.

"What about your *Amma*, Ram..." she enquired again.

Then I opened my mind. It was a long soliloquy like one in *Hamlet* – one of the four great tragedies of *Shakespeare*.

"My *Amma* too struggled a lot like you. But her struggle was entirely different from yours.... *Acchan* left us all alone. He left us only his debts and irresponsible deeds. He didn't take any responsibilities as a husband or father. I don't know for whose sake he married my poor *Amma*. She was quite pretty in those days – like you. *Ammumma* used to say about *Amma* she couldn't understand that man. The term 'understanding' is quite difficult to implement between a husband and a wife. Women don't melt for money. They melt in respect, care, and love. Understanding others is a rare skill. Even after years of togetherness, a married couple may not truly know each other – just like what happened to your husband. But there are some people, even acquaintances from a short period, who become close very fast. We can understand them better. But God does not permit us to live with them. God should not be blamed – it's our fate that prevents us. I haven't felt any attachment to him as a father. The absence of a father is truly a loss in a son's life. Sometimes I longed for love from a father. But that loss was not really a loss for me because *Amma* and *Ammumma* showered me with love and care, and my maternal uncles also cared for me a lot. I don't actually know what the duties of a father are? or his role in a boy's life? As far as I believe, a mother's love is unconditional, while all others ~ including a father's – are conditional. A mother is a truth. The loss of a father can be compensated by a mother. But the absence of a mother is real loss ~ we are truly alone without a mother. We are alone on this planet Earth." I abruptly stopped.

"Ram, your mother is really a great person. *Ammumma* too. What she is called, your *Ammumma?*" Gouri *Amma* asked.

"*Bhagirathi* is her name ~ one of the tributaries of river *Ganges*, the holy river as far as we are concerned. The river *Ganges* begins its flow from *Gangotri*. There, the *Ganges* is known as *Bhagirathi*. The very name, *Bhagirathi* is associated with *Bhagirathan* – a mythological character who struggled and starved to bring *Ganges* down to Earth to attain salvation for his ancestors – 60,000 in number. Even nowadays, there is an oft-quoted idiom in Malayalam: "*Bhageeratha prayathnam*" – a term used to denote strenuous and relentless effort. *Ammumma believed* in the nobility of education, and she, along with my grandfather, sent me to school. *Achachan* – my grandfather, as he was called, was a gem of character. His name was Raman Nair. He gave me the name Raghav. *Ammumma* is like holy water to me," I said with a sigh.

Ammumma is well-versed in astrology and occult studies. Her prophecy about me:

"When Radhasree brought you into this family, you were only five. We never learned your real date or place of birth, and without the exact time, any prediction is merely a guess. But one thing is certain: you must have a strong Jupiter in your horoscope. That is why fate brought you to us."

Raghav sighed bitterly.

"Is it all true?" Gouri *Amma* asked, astonished.

"Don't know. What might our future be? We don't really know," I replied.

"You do one thing -- please look up the horoscope of my Ganesh, dear. It's a request, "Gouri *Amma's* eyes filled with tears.

"Yeah, sure *Amma*. Don't worry" I said.

Ganesh's Horoscope and its impact

In the same year, I returned home on the eve of Thrissur Pooram, which falls in *Medam* – Aries, probably during second week of April. I approached *Ammumma* and told her everything about Ganesh and her mother, *Gouri Amma*. *Ammumma* was very pleased and listened intently, without any comments like a tree in stillness. She didn't respond immediately and only said, "Let me look into it and I will tell you during the next *brahmamuhurtha*."

"When is the *brahmamuhurtha*? ~ "I asked earnestly

"The next *brahmamuhurtha* will be early tomorrow morning, from 3:00 a.m. to 5: a.m. If you wake up, I will tell you everything about Ganesh, right? Please give me his horoscope." *Ammumma* asked.

I handed over Ganesh's horoscope, which was written on palm leaves in a unique way. It was tied and knotted with a yellow-coloured string.

Ammumma just observed it for a while, then began chanting some mantras to Lord Ganesh. She closed her eyes for a moment and glanced at the horoscope through her horn-rimmed spectacles. One could see her eyes appear doubled through the lenses. Gradually she began to speak:

"Raghav, this boy, who too is born during the *brahmamuhurta,* is a scholar by birth. His ascendant falls on Gemini, where Mercury is placed freely and independently. Mercury gives him intelligence, higher studies, good communication, and strong followers."

"His second house is Cancer, where the Sun and Rahu are conjoined ~ that is unfortunate. His father and mother separated during his early childhood. There is estrangement between them even now. The figure of his father is completely absent from his life. Rahu gives him knowledge of a foreign language."

"His third house is Leo, where Saturn and Jupiter are again conjoined. Sometimes this is favourable, sometimes not. His mind is always turbulent. It expands and contracts vehemently. He won't have any siblings. The Jupiter-Saturn conjunction in Leo is complex with both positive and negative outcomes. It is strong and well-placed. This union may also bring wealth and enjoyment in life. He will possess a strong optimistic mind."

The fourth house of Ganesh is Virgo, where Mars is placed alone. Mars gives him an aggressive nature. He is quarrelsome with his mother. But in his heart, she is his only destiny and soulmate. He constantly thinks of his mother's predicament regarding his father and her sorrowful nature.

His fifth house corresponds to Libra, – where the Moon is positioned very positively. In Vedic Astrology, the Moon signifies an emotional person with a creative mind. Like the scales in the symbol of Libra, they are hypersensitive and have a wavering mind. He will have intuitive powers, and sometimes can foresee his own future. He is very feminine in nature ~ that is, he is equally attracted to both women and men. He may also find joy in parenting or working with children.

In Ganesh's eighth house, Ketu stands alone in Capricorn. It's an earthly sign. This placement also indicates a strong interest in spirituality. He has a deep inclination towards mystical studies. It also indicates a past-life connection to spiritual practices and a high potential for spiritual awakening. This placement creates a genuine interest in social services and human welfare. He is honest from the core of this heart.

The twelfth house of Ganesh is Taurus, where Venus is placed alone. This is auspicious as Venus is in its own sign, making it fairly strong and beneficial. However, Venus here also indicates some hidden relationships. It indicates attraction to or success in foreign lands, including travel and settlement. And ...he is not attracted to women, but to men...."

"What ....!!!" I exclaimed.

"Yes, Raghav. This is the unsettling prediction from the horoscope," *Ammumma* said reluctantly.

"That might be the reason. Now I can understand his ambition to go abroad." I whispered to myself.

After my weekend holidays, I returned to Bangalore. That week I had a great deal of pending work at the office. I was eagerly waiting for a chance to meet Ganesh alone. But I couldn't find a favourable time to talk to him. Moreover, during the pooja holidays, they had a number of guests at home.

Next Sunday, I booked tickets for a Bollywood movie, planned as a way to get Ganesh alone. Fortunately, he agreed. I deliberately planned a movie based on a queer theme.

The film begins on a light note, filled with a lot of hilarious situations at first. Ganesh was talkative and excited in the theatre. But once the main theme was introduced, he became silent and focused.

The plot revolves around a gay policeman, and a lesbian teacher. They agree to marry to appease their families and avoid societal pressure. As they navigate their individual relationships and the challenges of their unconventional marital union, they gradually come to deeper understanding of themselves and each other.

The film explores the themes of LGBTQ, societal pressures on relationships, and the importance of self-acceptance and authenticity.

When the movie ended, I glanced at Ganesh's face. He smiled at me vaguely, then clasped my hands tightly and confessed reluctantly. "Raghav, I am ..."

I just cut off the talk and told him "I know "I deliberately held his hands tightly and continued, "Ganesh, I respect your orientation. I already knew from *Ammumma* – she is a well-versed astrologer. At least you confessed to me. That matters most. But you can tell me everything, can't you? Do you have a partner now?"

"Yes," Ganesh said. At that moment, his face bloomed like a red rose. Actually, that simile doesn't quite capture his expression.

"Who's that lucky fellow? I mean..." I asked earnestly.

"Like in the movie, he is a gay cop," Ganesh replied.

"When and how did it happen, dear?" I asked anxiously.

"He was my close companion and roommate during my postgraduation at IIT, Vadodara. He was desperately in search for a job. An orphan, he was adopted by an Anglo-Indian family at the age of fifteen. We stayed in the hostel together as roommates for two years. Sometimes he visited my home during vacations and Diwali holidays. *Amma* knows Madhav well. But she doesn't know anything about this. Being from an orthodox family, she wouldn't accept it, Raghav. When I looked at her face, I feel a pang. For me, she is everything. Without her, I am alone, Raghav. I couldn't confess to her that I am gay. How can I confess and possibly shatter all her aspirations with a single revelation? I am fed up, Raghav, by concealing every moment of my love for Madhav,". He said as tears streamed down his face.

When he mentioned the name Madhav, my mind went to my village and my childhood friend. I longed for his presence and his face. "Madhav.... Madhav..." I uttered again and again.

"Yes... my Madhav...my *Kanaya* – Lord Krishna, my life, my spirit ...." Ganesh repeated.

My memory glides from past to present in a fleeting minute. I craved Madhav's friendship – my guide and mentor during boyhood. Suddenly, his face appeared to my mind, smiling. His saffron attire and sweat always had that fragrance of sandalwood.

"Raghav...... Ram.... what are you thinking about? "Ganesh asked, touching me eagerly.

"Nothing more...... I had a friend named Madhav during my childhood. He met with a premature death. I just thought of him... sorry dear," I replied

"Oh... sorry, Ram," Ganesh said.

"How did your Madhav look? Was he good in appearance?" Ganesh asked curiously.

"Yes, my Madhav was my soulmate.... my close friend, my brother, and my guide. Like the bond between Lord Krishna and Arjuna. We played, ate, and slept together from first standard onwards. We even shared lunch together. His favourite was *curd rice*. Till 10th standard, we were in the same school. After SSLC, with his advice, I joined the Humanities group for pre-degree, while he went away for his higher studies. Then we had some correspondence in the form of letters. Thereafter there was no news about him. Then came the news of his death. I entered a state of depression after that. What happened to him? I don't know. Why didn't he tell me about his struggles? Only God knows." My eyes welled up with tears. I couldn't speak further. Ganesh gently patted my shoulder and said, "No, Ram. I didn't know the name Madhav meant so much to you."

"It's okay, Ganesh. If someone asked me what kind of friend I want, I'll say one who never changes from the day we meet until the last breath. That was Madhav. I forgot all my worries, when I would spend time with Madhav. One beautiful friend is better than a thousand beautiful faces."

"I don't think there's anything in life more beautiful than having people who make you feel emotionally secure and safe. Is it not? Ganesh? Sometimes, the two people who are truly meant for each other must overcome greatest obstacles just to be together." I said.

"Yes, dear Ram, you said it well. Don't worry so much about friendship, dear. Instead of your Madhav, I will be with you for this entire life span. See how fate has been played so beautifully with the name Madhav. We two are together with a single name, 'Madhav'. Take my Madhav as your friend and give Madhav as my partner, right? You don't need to worry about love and friendship. It is all around you, every day, in every moment. It can reach you at your best and it will meet you at your worst. There is nothing in this world stronger than love and friendship. Love is the music you are listening to, the jokes you create, and the way you always return. It's a two-way communication. Sometimes love is an emotion in the form of exchanges like 'Are you fine, dear?' or 'Did you take your food?' or 'Is it raining there' or 'Did you get wet?' or 'Did you reach home safely?' or..."

Ganesh was excited and tapped my cheeks. Then he continued again. "There might be a universal law. The universe will keep two people apart until the timing is right. When both of them finally meet, there will be so many coincidences and mysterious things happening. But they would have never crossed paths. This universe itself aligns, and they will realize everything they just went through before they met was preparing their hearts for each other. One day, when you least expect it, you are going to spark with someone who is going to be so soft and gentle with your heart, and you are going to be so glad you kept it open."

"How far have both of you become entangled, Ganesh?" I asked curiously.

"Well, it happened in those old hostel days itself, at the initial stage of our post-graduation. He was like a complete stranger to me those days. We didn't speak much, only the necessary exchanges. Gradually it happened. For me, I didn't have a good friend-cum-listener in my life. I longed for a good listener. I wanted to talk about many things, especially the absence of my father. The weeping face of my mother used to haunt me from my childhood. If you are feeling frustrated, impatient, or constantly waiting for something to finally happen, remember that things tend to unfold right when they are supposed to and not a moment sooner.

I got tired of explaining myself to people who never really listened. No matter how honest I was, they still made it seem like I was wrong. But in Madhav I found a good friend and a good listener. But in the meantime, I loved him wholly."

"During my childhood my father used to beat me and my mother brutally. What is the reason we two don't know even now. One day he expelled the two of us and asked my mother to go home from Bangalore. Those days we were settled in an interior landscape surrounded by dense forest. That day I couldn't forget. Even on a rainy day I couldn't sleep; sometimes I used to wake up with loud cries and search for a picture of Lord Krishna, usually hung on the wall of my ancestral home. But in the hostel, I couldn't find a solution. I woke up restlessly and just lay beside his bed side. Gradually he became quite aware of this and he accompanied me to sleep. That was my first sign of friendship.

I found in him a father, friend and a partner. When I place my head on his chest, I felt secure. A feeling of belongingness was whispered in the form of his heartbeat. It is not merely physical, Ram – it is, for the most part, emotional." Ganesh told with a sigh and completed his vast monologue like Tennyson's *Ulysses*.

Again, he asked me with a curious tone, "Ram, is it a big mistake on my part? My orientation is like this by birth. So, I couldn't find anything wrong in it, dear. But when I think about my *Amma* I feel a pang in my heart. How can I disclose these things to her? I don't know what might be my future. Madhav is too anxious about all these things, dear. He cut himself off from the masses three years ago. Neither his parents nor his relatives accepted this. *Amma* is expecting a lot and she is anxiously waiting for a girl for me. No... Ram I couldn't tolerate the same. I couldn't.... It is a cruel thing. How can I...Ram...dear! I couldn't.... It is one of the worst forms of betrayal that a person has ever done, right? I long for a male partner not a female one. Even in the bedside also. I couldn't imagine a woman nearby my side. Ah...!"

"Ganesh, there is nothing wrong in it. First of all, you have to accept your orientation. That is a part of your life and destiny. We can't change that reality. Accept people as they are. As far as your mother is concerned, it's a grave issue. That is the main thing in it. That matters much, right? See, a country like India doesn't accept this kind of relationship." I told him and made him confident enough.

"Ram, that is why we two will migrate to the Netherlands or somewhere in the European countries," Ganesh said abruptly this time.

When I heard about Netherlands, I thought about Gouri *Amma* once telling me about Ganesh's intention to settle abroad. Now I understood Ganesh's intention for going abroad, especially to the European continent, where the ecstasy of gaydom is celebrated and legalised.

"Ram...Ram... what are you thinking about?" Ganesh prompted me to speak again.

"Ganesh, what about your mother? Do you think she will accept all this? I don't know about it. She is badly in need of a daughter-in-law and what you return back ...oh! God! Krishna! Govinda! How will she accept these types of things. I don't know... She struggled a lot for your sake from your father and family. Now she is living only for your sake also and how could she accept this? May be this too is the reality of fate, right? Why is God's judgement too vicious to come down to our level? If he is loving, why does He judge His fellows so harshly? Giving so much pain and worry – trials and tribulations." I whispered to Ganesh as a reply and continued again.

"*Ammumma* sometimes told us in the midst of the advice by Krishna to Arjuna in the eve of the great battle, Arjuna asks Krishna, "When does the universe test us the most, Oh! Keshav? The reply was sometimes the universe tests you the most and badly when you are very close to a new chapter in life. Such is the case of your mother "

“So, what shall I do? Shall I commit suicide?... Tell me... “Ganesh retorted angrily.

“No dear, never do such a heinous action. I just made a confession about your mother. Your orientation is not your choice, right? When I thought about your mother’s face, I just expressed my views spontaneously, that’s it. You needn’t worry about that. See, mothers are the ones who love us unconditionally. The rest of others’ love for us is conditional, Ganesh. Even a father’s love is sometimes conditional, you know? That’s the relation of umbilical cord. *Ammumma* used to say about this relationship between a mother and her baby. In my opinion, Ganesh, mothers will always give more importance than fathers. She gave birth to you which cannot be done by a father. The pain she tolerated during the birth of a baby is so intense, Ganesh. Such a pain even a father cannot tolerate. Her endurance and sufferings... bringing a child into its life path itself is really a sacrifice, dear. The patriarchal system of our world never appreciates her sacrifice. Society is highly male-dominated, Ganesh. Now we are living in the 21st century, the century of technology and science – the computer era of growth and prosperity. The age of social networks, the age of transformations, the age of Artificial Intelligence (AI), the age of controversies. It’s the middle part of the *Kali Yuga* – the age of riots, violence, disappointments and disillusions. It is the last of the four epochs in Hindu cosmology and it is highly characterized by a decline in morality, spirituality and social harmony. Essentially, it is often considered an age of darkness and suffering, but also a time of opportunity for spiritual and material growth. According to the *Bhagavad Gita*, living a righteous and fulfilling life in *Kali Yuga* involves embracing truth, righteousness, love and peace. In your case your love is your destiny. It is not the first thing in this world. If you are happy with your partner – male or female – it's okay. The happiness in this age matters. May be this relation is your way out, not a hide out, right? So go on with that, dear. But one thing, according to me, you have to bring your mother along with you. That is my sincere advice to you. Without you she couldn't survive. Poor thing." I stopped my long talk with a sigh again.

"*Amma* won't come with me, Ram," Ganesh told me.

"That's not your headache, Ganesh. That's solely mine, leave it for me. I will make her agree, don't worry," I said, trying to reassure him.

"*Amma* has a special liking to you. She aways talks about you and your *Ammumma* and *Amma* in Kerala." Ganesh said.

"That's why I am telling you ~ never let her eyes be wet with tears, dear," I told him.

"Deal, Ram. If I have another birth in this age, we must be born in the same womb. Today is Mother's Day, Ram. Please convey my regards and loving hugs to your mother. Tell her one more thanks because she gave me such a wonderful friend like you. You are the most precious gem in my life. You are my guide, Ram. Now I can understand the meaning of the word 'FRIEND'."

Ganesh hugged me tightly and his eyes filled with tears. I gently wiped them. "I will always be with you, right? Don't worry. The road you have selected in this long run is less travelled. So, challenges are part of it. Be aware and careful of society and the people around you. So, you three – Madhav, you, and your mother – must go away for a far cry, right? Very far.... a safe place. And live happily with Madhav, like your laugh ~ full of dreams, "I said.

The very next day, I approached Gouri *Amma*. After establishing a rapport, I began my talk about Ganesh and Madhav. She couldn't speak at first. She passively listened to everything I told her about the love between Madhav and her son. I tried to convince her that whoever our partner may be, he or she should be a good human being first – not judged by gender or colour. Then I continued,

"Gouri *Amma*, if it doesn't happen, we might lose Ganesh forever. That would be a heavy blow for us. Let him live happily with his partner Madhav. It's not a crime. It's in accordance with his orientation. It is in his blood. We can't get rid of it with treatment and medicine. It is part of his personality. Otherwise, we will lose him forever".

"But Ram, I had so many expectations for Ganesh, dear, I am at a loss now. I expected so much! His marriage, a daughter-in-law, children..." Gouri *Amma* whimpered.

"*Amma*, take it in good sense. And what do all these marriage and children mean anyway? A horrible adjustment ~ you know that well from your life. Leave it.

You are a woman; that's why you suffered a lot. But let Ganesh live his own life in this universe."

"Yes, that's true... Probably he got fed up with all those things. From my life he must have learned how to get rid of such obstacles --adjustment, liabilities and all. Yes, poor child. Tell him, Ram...I fully agree with him, because at least he should stay alive before my eyes. He will be happy with my support. I am happy..." Gouri *Amma* cried again and tried to wipe her tears with the loose end of her saree.

"*Amma*...accept his wish fully and wholeheartedly, right? *Ammumma* used to tell me that we are born on this earth for a purpose. A particular reason lies behind our birth. We must patiently wait for the moment to fulfil our aim. More than anything, we should do our *Karma* well - that is our prime duty. Whatever your happiness or sorrows, triumphs and disasters, all are based on your *Karmas* from previous births. In this *Kali Yuga*, one must be spiritually aware. These days, marriage is often a matter of convenience. You know, in the Western world, the culture of single motherhood is increasing day by day. In *Kali Yuga*, women are highly educated and professional. Unlike you, Gouri *Amma*, who waited a lifetime for love from your husband, women today don't want to wait for a mahout to control and correct them. They are empowered and self-reliant. They seek emotional warmth from the man they love –it's not merely physical, as men often believe. The men are, sometimes, highly materialistic. They need a woman like a toy princess in a toy world. Whenever the men turn the switch on, the toy princess should dance or run. That is the reality today. Even in films, what is the theme? In films we can always watch that women are the instruments to receive love from men. First love begins from a man, then he approaches a woman to receive his love. She reluctantly accepts. When a woman approaches a man at first for her love that film will be a flop, right. That is the reality of our country. Men and Women are the two sides of a same coin. That is our prime concern. But in this country that reality is fully wiped off. Here society is controlled by menfolk. They are framing the culture, laws and reign. Marriage sometimes turns out to be horrible. It is more of a compromise. It is women who always suffer in marriage, especially in a patriarchal society like this. "I stopped my long soliloquy abruptly.

"Ram, don't worry I agree with Ganesh and Madhav," Gouri *Amma* said.

"Yes. As I told you, this country is not ready for this kind of relationship. So, Gouri *Amma* should go with them abroad." I said.

"Abroad? Where...?" Gouri *Amma* asked curiously.

"To somewhere in the Western world..." I replied.

"It's okay...I will go with them... Both are my children, right?" Gouri *Amma* said abruptly.

Six months passed. I stayed with Ganesh and Gouri *Amma* for a long time without returning home. *Amma* and *Ammumma* were much worried about me. I made my mind confident enough to bid them farewell to New Zealand.

The day before their taking off to the airport, I helped them to pack the things and arranged everything.

The time of departure was near. In the early morning at 2:00 am., we left home and reached the airport by 3:00 am. At the airport, I saw Madhav first. He was much a well-built man with a strong masculine figure. He was much taller than Ganesh. We met in front of the parking area. Gouri *Amma* clasped my hand, and together we walked towards the main arena. There was a long queue of passengers. We waited for around half an hour. At last, our turn came. The three of them showed their passports, visas, and travel insurance at the gate. They were allowed to enter. I just bid them farewell by waving my hand. Both of them Ganesh and Madhav came towards me and shook hands. I told them "All the best, dear. Take care of my Gouri *Amma* too, alright? Her medicines and her health."

Then they went inside. I stood behind the barricade and watched them. They were heading towards the long escalator. I gazed at them until they vanished from my sight. Gouri *Amma* kept looking at me, until she got onto the escalator. I did the same. She was not able to get on by herself. Madhav turned and held her close, while the escalator moved. Ganesh also helped him. I was deeply touched by the sight. Then they disappeared from view. I wiped my tears too. Entering the home after their departure was unbearable. I felt an emptiness in Ganesh's home. Without Gouri *Amma*, the kitchen and corridors felt completely vacant. I couldn't tolerate the emptiness any longer. They gave me the house keys and instructed me to stay there as long as my job in Bangalore continued. I stayed there for two days. I miss Gouri *Amma* and Ganesh so much that I cannot express it. Ever and never. Both of them are truly close to my heart.

That night, sleep eluded me. My thoughts drifted to my *Amma* and my *Ammumma*, and to Gouri *Amma* – how many hardships and quiet sacrifices they endured to raise me and Ganesh. Without a woman, a home feels hollow. How much labour a woman undertakes within a family – endless household work, borne without pay or recognition. I bow my head in reverence to every mother in the universe.

Saga of Raghav

The very next day, I left Bangalore. In the midst of such predicaments, I craved relationships. In such moments, going home seemed the only solution to clear my mind. I reached home at night. *Ammumma* was waking up in order to receive me. *Ammumma* once again was in a hurry to eat the beetle leaves and waiting to spit out and asked me "What's wrong with you...my child..."

"No...nothing serious..." I replied.

"But your face is rather pale, and it seems as though you are starved. Did you take anything at noon?" *Ammumma* inquired.

"No, *Amma*...I want to bathe in the pond. Let me bathe in the pond. I want to swim for a while. It makes me fresh, right? "I said.

"Time is 8 o' clock, it's rather late now and cloudy. There is a glimpse of rain also. You must have it tomorrow. Now you can take your bath here only, right? Good boy, dear. I have already prepared some hot water for you. Then what else? What about the news of Gouri *Amma* and Ganesh? All is well at time." *Ammumma* asked again.

"They left Bangalore and went to the Netherlands," I told *Ammumma.*

"Oh! So sudden. All of a sudden. I was not informed of this. What happened?" *Ammumma* asked.

"He got a job there and I insisted his mother go with him. That's it." I replied.

"It's good news. *Krishna.... Yogeshwar....* protect that mother and child dear...*Narayana...Narayana....*" *Ammumma* chanted and went to her room.

Amma came then. "Did you take the bath?" *Amma* asked.

"No...not yet," I replied

"Then make it fast. I will serve your food when you return," *Amma* said.

"*Amma*, what's the curry for today?" I asked.

"Nothing special. Usual boiled rice with sambar that has been made of small onions and grounded coconut – your favourite, I know. Then the pickle of tender mangoes. Then curd is there. I have also prepared some *papads*." *Amma* told.

"Yes *Amma.* I will be back in a minute, just like a crow-bath, right?" I replied and rushed to the bath room.

After my bath, when I entered the kitchen, *Amma* was waiting there at the dining table for me. At once she poured some rice and sambar into the steel plate. Pickle was poured into a small dish.

As I took the first handful of rice, I told her, " *Amma*...I really miss all these days. Talking with Gouri *Amma*, I don't know...how much she struggled, right? When I heard about Gouri *Amma*'s whole story I really missed you *Amma*...Even though I am not your son by blood, I was brought up by you so carefully. Your position is above God in my mind *Amma*..." I clasped *Amma's* hand with my left hand and brought it towards my lips, those morsel-filled lips, and touched it. Tears came from my eyes. I cried bitterly. *Amma* asked, "What's wrong with you...crying...in front of the food...it's not good, dear...Raghav...Raghav."

She wiped the tears from my eyes neatly with her *Anchol* of her saree and told me again, "Finish your food first...Then we can talk about it in detail, right?"

Again, I picked up the rice and mixed it with the sambar. I couldn't take it again. There was a pain in my throat. When *Amma* persisted, I reluctantly continued the process of filling my stomach.

After finishing my food, I approached my mother. She was cleaning the kitchen table and plates. I am waiting for her. I wanted to talk to her about many things - about myself and my roots. Why did she adopt me in this chaotic world? What is the reason for my upbringing without being selfish? She didn't care about her life even today. She, along with *Ammumma*, has showered a lot of love and care upon me. They made me think that this is my family and I am one among them. No one in this family discriminated me as an orphan child. Even the uncles and aunts also cared for and protected me. I was thinking of all those things again and again. Some vague memories are still in my mind but not precise. A shadow of a fatherly figure but not sorted out. A tall man with a long and husky moustache. His eyes had a reddish colour. His voice was too husky. His angry face. A brawl scene and violence followed. I slept for a long time and after my tiresome journey I woke up and found my *Amma*. Before that, the face of another woman whom I think is also remembered. What happened to me in the midst of that violence? No idea. So, I had a mother, who was mine by blood. She was murdered by that angry faced father. Then I was brought up by this new mother. That's all. I know nothing more than that. Anyhow, at least I have a mother, right? Whether she is surrogative or true - she treated me all these years as her own child. So, by Karma she is my real mother. I taught my mind like this till today.

"Raghav..." *Amma* called.

"Yes...! I'm just trying to remember those things." I replied.

"For what...what happened to you...Gouri *Amma*'s story is mind- breaking to you, and don't you know what is your mother's story?" *Amma* asked.

"Actually, I don't want to remember all those things. But now you are curious to learn them. Now you are thirty. At least you should have attained stability in your mind. The first thing is that I am not your mother - that you know clearly. But don't think about that truth deeply." *Amma* continued.

"We are two children for your *Ammumma*. My father only inherited five cents of land along with a dilapidated home. Actually, that home was a cowshed in olden days, that was beside the ancestral home. Being very straight forward and honest, my *Acchan* – your grandfather – didn't ask anything from the partition. But they should have given him, because he did many things for the family. More than, that he had two children. But they didn't give him anything except this cowshed. *Acchan* modified this cowshed into a home. It is one-storied. During the rainy season, the so-called monsoon showers, the rain water seeps through the narrow holes of tiles and we were engaged every time to fill the holes with *arecanut spathe*. *Acchan* was very strict in his dealings with children. I am the second one by birth. The elder brother studied well. After SSLC he secured high marks and went to a polytechnic college at Thrissur. But there was a shadow of poverty still existing. In those days women were not permitted to study higher. My father didn't want to educate daughters further. When a woman attained the age of eighteen, the essential thing was to settle down with her marriage. That was the main thing. But I had great dreams. I used to dance well. I wanted to study more. Especially arts were my passion. I used to read English and Malayalam novels. Especially poems and fictions were my favourite. I liked the poems of Sarojini Naidu and Toru Dutt. The lines I often remember by Sarojini Naidu from a poem – "*Songs of Radha*". Radha's desperate search for her lover Krishna, reflecting the themes of divine love and devotion are found in these lines:

"All night my heart its lonely vigil kept

Listening for thee, O Love. All night I wept

Where went they wanton footsteps wandering,

Sweet Ghanashyam, my King?"

Radha – the lover of Krishna – had a far-fetching effect upon my mind. I admire her, her true love for Krishna. Sometimes I identified with Radha herself. Radha's quest for love is not only the quest of Radha herself but also the quest of entire womanhood, you know. Fickle-minded men never know what the true love of a woman is. They are rather material. Women need emotional warmth and care; that is not the way men think. "*Amma* sighed and continued.

"Once *Ammumma* told me after reading my horoscope, your star *Vishakam* is the star of Radha – the lover of Krishna. So, you have to wait for years to receive your love's concern. Like Radha, who was waiting for Krishna for a whole life, your life is like hers. No way to change your destiny. You have the yoga of second marriage too, dear child. She used to say all these things to father also. But being a rationalist, he didn't give ear to the same." *Amma* reluctantly stopped the conversation, and she gazed at me to say, "Raghav, you are thirty now. This is a question from my heart, right. If I were your true mother by blood, I couldn't have asked this sort of silly question, right?" She smiled, with a blush in her face.

"Have you experienced true love?"

"No, not yet. I had a lot of girlfriends in college days. But neither of them suited for a true love. Only for time's sake. That's all. Once in post graduate days, I remember, but it ended up with her marriage. She was not serious as well. So, no problem" I said.

"I too had a love story, Raghav. From childhood onwards we were in the knot of love – true love what I called it. It has a beautiful climax of waiting as I still wait for him...!" *Amma* sighed.

"You are still waiting for him..." I enquired

"Yes, Raghav, I still..." *Amma* said boldly.

"Who is that lucky guy?" I asked anxiously.

Amma smiled and said, "*Poda*...it's not like your post graduate love story. This I hereby tell you is a true love story. I first saw Govind in temple as he was a regular visitor and an ardent devotee of goddess Durga – divine feminine energy and often depicted as a warrior riding a lion to slay demons. The sanctum sanctorum of the temple would be closed for the major service of *Deeparadhana*. Both of us would stand there, folding our hands in obeisance. While standing there, he would turn back on and off, to see me. The priest would bring the plate full of holy ash after the holy service inside the sanctum sanctorum. It would be Govind who would take the plate and circle it around his face. Then, it would be my turn. This continued during my ninth and tenth grades. Those were the golden moments in my life. First love we couldn't forget in our life till our last breath. As far as women are concerned, they couldn't forget the same. I had started to wear saree in those days. But Govind always wanted me to wear *setmundu*. After my SSLC I used to take tuitions for the neighbouring students. I just did the tuitions only to brush up my general knowledge for attending PSC exams. Anyhow each student gave me Rs. 30/-. Altogether I saved 700 or 750 per month. During Onam season I collected the coins in an earthen pot and bought a beautiful shirt for Govind. He too gave me garden saree in return. That saree I still have kept in my almirah. Raghav, one thing you should keep in mind that - when I died you just cover my corpse with that beautiful garden saree."

Amma suddenly began to weep lifting the edge of her *anchal* to wipe her tears.

"*Amma*...what's wrong with you. Your love is so intense even though you attained the age of fifty-eight. It's really mind-breaking. Is he still there in Thrissur?" I asked with a sigh of anxiety.

"Hmm.... He is still here. Now alone in an antique house. I heard about him from the maid servant Paru. Paru told me that he used to ask about me and you. Sometimes he asked Paru whether Raghav had any intention of marriage. So that he wanted to come into my life again. He is wistfully waiting." *Amma* said.

"*Amma*... then what happened to your love and tell me why you separated?" I asked enquiringly.

"Like all our love stories fate is the main villain. In this case Govind's father didn't like our love. He was of the opinion that Nair is inferior to Brahmins. In those days Brahmin supremacy was so intense. My father also found a man for my marriage. A man of wild behaviour, a man of cruelty and sadism. We didn't have a choice of our own in those days. Even without our consent marriage happens. Thus, my father ended my love story with a pang," *Amma* said.

"All of a sudden...*Amma* didn't inform Govind about your marriage?" I asked earnestly.

"I cried a lot and not knowing what to do? Apart from being grief-stricken, what shall I do in this case? All were against us. He didn't have so much courage to elope with me. More than that I yielded to my *Acchan's* advice. But he made me understand about Govind and their proud inheritance. *Acchan* told me that you haven't so much fortune to get Govind. For your sake I will talk to Govind's father but I am not sure whether he agrees" *Amma* said.

"What happened then..." I asked

"I cried and cried. In those days I used to light lamp at the *Sarpakavu*. Mostly in every ancestral home woman or female children should do that custom. I continuously carried a full silver glass of milk for the snake deity for nine days for fulfilling my wish to have Govind in my life as husband. One day a huge cobra came from the woods of the *Sarpakavu* and drank the whole milk from the silver glass. After finishing the drinking, it looked at me with its hood. I prayed and bowed to and asked it not to separate me from Govind. It wistfully and silently glanced at me with its hood. I just approached it and gave my right hand to the cobra and asked it to bite me. But at once it returned back to the *kavu*. I called it again and again and asked it to bite...it was of no use. I cried and my voice echoed in the *kavu*. 'Please take me through a bite from this earth..." *Amma* said desperately.

"Didn't you see Govind all these days *Amma*?" I asked.

"No, I didn't see him ...Day before my marriage – the falling of that holy thread ceremony – Paru gave me a letter. It was the first and last letter I got from Govind. That letter too I have kept even now in the same *almirah*, where I kept the saree," *Amma* said reluctantly.

"You wait here." She made for her room and returned within a minute with a letter in her hand. The letter had been folded. Its colour was vermilion yellow, even though it had been kept carefully. *Amma* handed over the letter to me. I just unfolded it; the letters were written in blue ink.

My Radhasree,

It's been a long time since I saw you at the temple. Each day I have been waiting for you, Radha. Without you, I am alone, dear. I can't live without you.

I want to talk to you, Radha, about a lot of things. Due to commitments and responsibilities, I couldn't make a decision,

Radha. But in my life, I won't wait for another woman. I will drink life to the drowsy lees as a single man. I don't accept life as a second chance. If you want to come with me, no problem. We can go away from this cursed village, that won't give anything to either of us.

I have so much to tell you, Radha...a whole lot of innumerable things...You need not respond...just sit and listen. What we discussed all these years has become more like chaff, I think. I have a lot more to share.

If you want to talk and live with me for a whole life, come the next day at Sarpakavu at 12:00 a.m right. If I won't come, think that I am dead, right.

I miss you a lot. Please stay careful, and never be sad, because I love to see your smiling face.

Come without fail,

Yours,

Govind

"This was the first and last letter from Govind" *Amma* sighed.

"Amme.... then what happened...?" I asked anxiously

"As per the instruction in the letter, I prepared to go to the *kavu* at 9.00 p.m. But it was the eve of my marriage. Everyone was running to and fro. I was anxiously waiting for a chance to go to the *kavu.* Then an unnatural rain started falling. Such a rain I had never seen in my life. I have already packed my belongings in a tiny bag. I kept my store of coins in the earthen pot inside the bag. I took *Acchan's* old umbrella and waited for the time to go," *Amma* continued with a whimper.

"When I saw everyone around at home, I felt disgusted with myself for having such a fate ~ to elope with someone of my own will. Had my *Acchan* given permission for my alliance with Govind, this would not have happened, right? But what a fate I possessed. I had to take the decision alone. I couldn't even reveal this secret to a single family member. The time was moving very fast that night. It was still raining in the hills ~ raining cats and dogs. Was nature too against my wishes and aspirations? I asked myself. The time was 11.00 p.m. When I looked at *Acchan's* face, I felt a pang. *Amma* and *Acchan* had prepared to sleep in the attic on an old wooden bed that was not fit for the two of them. I just entered the room. The light was rather dim. I touched both of their feet. Tears streamed from my eyes and fell on *Acchan's* feet. Then I immediately returned from the room and quickly made my way to the inner veranda along with the bag, that which I had kept in the *padippura*. Without looking back, I rushed to the *Sarpakavu*. Now the rain had lessened. Some slashes of rain still there. When I entered the *Sarpakavu*, I was fully surrounded by darkness. I couldn't see anything. The sound of the crickets frightened me."

The time was 11:45 now. I had to wait fifteen minutes more. Nearby, there was a motor shed. I entered the shed and lit a torch. That torch was given to *Acchan* by *Unniyettan*, who had recently returned from abroad –

Dubai. I was very fearful and hesitant to take that decision. My mind told me that when Govind came, everything would be okay. I have already told you; time was running too fast to control that day. Then came 12:00 am, 12:15 am, and finally 01:05 am. Every ten minutes I came out of the shed and looked around, but no trace of a human being was spotted. I was scared and rather confused. What to do? Where is Govind? Did he think I am alone here? How can I stay here all alone? I prayed to God for Govind's arrival. 'Hey...Govind, powerful Almighty, please let him come. Please come to me, *Yogeswar.* Hey.... *Krishna.... Krishna....* Govind...."

Amma again wiped her tears with the loose end of her saree and said, "Sometimes, someone walks into your life and changes everything. They raise your standards, give you strength, make you feel like yourself. There's something about them you can't even explain. And it scares you to lose them because deep down, you know you'll never find that feeling again" and continued.

"I heard footsteps outside, and my instincts took over. I stepped out of the shed, torch in hand, and flashed a signal into the darkness. The beam illuminated a face I knew all too well – *Acchan,* his eyes wild with desperation, his expression sending a shiver down my spine."

As I braced myself for *Acchan's* anger, his demeanour underwent a surprising transformation. His voice, once stern, now dripped with a deep sadness.

"Dear child', he whispered, his words laced with a mix of gratitude and pain. "I've been waiting for Govind, right here, near your shed. When I saw you come to touch my feet, it was as if time stood still. I felt a sudden jolt, and a wetness seeped into my consciousness. That's when I decided to follow you, unseen, my heart heavy with unspoken words".

"*Acchan's* voice was lipped with a quiet resolve, his eyes clouding over with a mix of pain and determination. "Govind is still missing, and I have held on to hope, for your sake, I know you loved him deeply, perhaps more than you ever loved me. But life has taken its own course, and now I must take a stand. You will marry the man I have chosen for you, and that is final. It's my last wish, and as your father, I expect you to obey. It is a debt I must pay, a duty I must fulfil, even if it breaks my heart". *Acchan* told me.

"Then my marriage. As per *Acchan's* instructions, both of them returned home. The time was around 05:05 a.m. Everybody was awake. All the people at home didn't face me. I was asked to bathe and get ready for the so-called auspicious marriage. I just went to the temple with my cousin sisters and prayed ardently. I didn't know what to pray for. Without Govind, my life wouldn't be complete. I have already made up my mind. I didn't know about that strange and forlorn man who was coming to marry me. Who might that strange and wild man be? Actually, what does it mean? In those days, we girls were not permitted to talk with boys of the same age. We were not allowed to go anywhere after 6:00 p.m. We were entrapped inside the home. We weren't allowed to go out or stay elsewhere. We were bound to home under the same roofs and walls. We were chained within the four inches of ivory. We were not even allowed to go outside the state for higher studies. I wanted to study more, especially in Dance. But higher studies were a forbidden fruit in those days. Gender bias existed throughout Kerala. Then what type of freedom are they talking about in marital harmony? Complete foolishness. Marriage is a failed institution. But its impact is rather vicious in India – the land of sages and saints. I don't know how a woman can live with a stranger, whom she meets for the first time only at tea-time.

When I returned from the temple, Paru told me that Govind and his friend had met with an accident the previous night when it was raining. His friend died on the spot, but Govind was heavily injured and admitted to the hospital. That news hit me like a hail in the mind. I was fully confused about the marriage. I longed for the marriage to be stopped. I wanted to be there with Govind in the hospital, to care for him. But what could I do? I had already promised *Acchan* about the marriage. Full of chaos...my life was at a standstill. Unable to move, I just sat at the bedside and wept."

Ammumma used to say about my horoscope that I have a debilitated Jupiter in the 8th house of Cancer. Cancer is the favourite place of Jupiter. But Jupiter in the 8th house is not good in a woman's horoscope. More than that, my first house lord is placed in Jupiter. Jupiter is the biggest planet in the solar system. But its position in the 8th bhava gives negative results, especially concerning, marital life. Overall, it's not a good position. The ascendant lord in the 8th house is unfavourable, and you may achieve everything in life after prolonged obstacles. But in my case, I was a bit lucky, as Jupiter is exalted in Cancer. Therefore, I would achieve everything in life, but only through difficulties. This Jupiter causes delays in decision making. This always keeps one confused. An exalted ascendant lord in the 8th house grants long life and comforts. But the long life is full of sorrows and worries. You might be highly religious and spiritual too. *Ammumma's* predictions were correct, as far as this loss of love is concerned". *Amma* again justified the ways of God towards man.

"*Ammumma* added one more thing. The day I intended to elope with Govind was '*Vinayaka Chathurthi*'. On that day, we are not supposed to look at the Moon. Why do we avoid looking at the moon on Ganesh on '*Vinayaka Chathurthi*'? According to the *Vrata Katha*, Lord Ganesha cursed the moon for mocking him, leading to false accusations for those who see it. As per the story, Lord Krishna was falsely accused of stealing the precious jewel *Syamantaka.* Sage Narada explained that this curse occurred because Krishna had sighted the moon on *Bhadrapada Shukla Chathurthi*. Since then, devotees avoid seeing the moon on this day." *Amma* again sighed.

When she told the story about Ganesha and the myth, I recollected the faces of Ganesh and Gouri Amma. Both of their faces were glaring in my mind. Gouri is a synonym of the name *Parvathy*. I was quite curious about my *Amma's* marital life and my own entrance into her life. Both still seem like a coincidence. Even life is sometimes a coincidence. "Man proposes, God disposes" is the apt quote for life. But life should still have some aim. I understand the love bond between *Amma* and Govind.

I asked *Amma* again, "Then what happened? Did you prepare for this marriage within such a short time?"

"No, it's an emphatic no. I saw the face of your father at that moment ~ when I bowed my head to wear the *thali*. That yellow-stained thread is actually a knot of a woman's dreams. It's a knot of assurance, the core of marital harmony. But that assurance I don't know whether it's a boon or a bane. No idea. "*Amma* said reluctantly.

"And what happened then?" I asked.

"My marriage was over that day. It was the full stop of everything in my life ~ you know – my studies, dreams, and aspirations. I didn't want to see that stranger's face. He was rather arrogant in appearance, with his long moustache and wild look. That very day, I didn't see him smile even once. He was tall, very tall ~ like a coconut tree," *Amma* said.

"Then..." I asked again.

"He didn't even allow me to stay there that wedding night. I was asked to go with him. After the ceremony, I was taken to that strange house. His parents were good. They spoke to me cordially. The events of the first night were quite mysterious. I didn't know what had happened to him. His behaviour was also quite wild. I waited for more than three hours in the bed chamber for him, holding a full glass of milk. But he didn't turn up. I was rather sleepy. Then he came walking unsteadily. His movements reminded me of a poem 'My *Papa's Waltz*' from my Pre-degree English text book. The poem begins:

"The whiskey on your breath

Could make a small boy dizzy;

But I hung on like death:

Such waltzing was not easy."

"He was waltzing like someone at a ballroom dance party. When he approached me and said "Wish... you. a. h...a...p... p...y. married life..." He fell like a giant tree. That was the end of my first night. I thought every marriage was like that."

"The very next day, I was ordered to pack my clothes and go with him. The destination of our journey was Mangalore in Karnataka. It wasn't a tour or honeymoon trip. He was working there as an estate supervisor as *Acchan* had told me. I wore the saree that has been given by the groom's family. It was green with a red border. I looked very beautiful that day in that saree. When a girl wears a saree, she looks more mature, right? I was my first trip boarding a train. My first experience of travelling by train. But we were in the general compartment. The train was heavily crowded. From Thrissur, we had to stand. When the train reached Kuttippuram, we got seats, but in different seats. I just saw his face – exactly like a villain in Bollywood movies. What was his name? I don't remember now. That man used to be the villain in all the Hindi movies at that time. I was hungry and thirsty but reluctant to ask him. In the train, all the men were looking at me because I was the only new bride, out there. Some looked at my face, others at my saree, and most women stared at my ornaments. Your *Ammumma* had given me 200 grams of gold in the form of ornaments. Most of them were chains, 10 bangles, and a *manga mala*. Altogether 200 grams. My brother gave me a wrist watch made in Japan.

When the train reached, Kasaragod we were seated close together. I asked him for some water, but he told me to wait, saying that the next stop would be our destination. When I stepped onto the soil of Mangalore, I was astounded by the railway station itself. That station was four times bigger than our Thrissur station. We took a bus from there. That bus too was heavily crowded. He didn't give me even a drop of water. The journey was tiresome. I was standing in the bus for more than one hour. It was the last stop. We couldn't call it a township. Only two or three shops were scattered here and there. People were highly illiterate; could tell at first glance. After that, he took a bullock cart. I was rather thirsty and hungry, about to vomit. From early morning onwards, I had neither eaten nor drunk anything. The journey in the cart was too tiresome. The jerking sound and the movement of the bulls irritated me. Finally, we reached a place. It seemed to me like a jungle after all ~ a thick, dense forest. The sound of crickets even in the day time frightened me. The sound of the streams and the roaring of tigers truly frightened me. What might be the structure of the house to which we were going? I didn't know. I was scared. Even in the midst of all these tensions, I longed for Govind and his face. What might the condition of Govind be now?"

"We were still walking ~ walking for walking's sake. Finally, we reached a place. It was actually a hut. A hut in the sense the roof was thatched. A one-roomed hut. When I entered the house, I again felt trauma. No electricity, no water. Some dishes and pots were scattered here and there. More than that, a stinging smell filled the air. He told me to bathe. But where? I didn't know. I asked him for some water. He told me to take water from the nearby stream. It was probably a half kilometre away. I just sat on the mat. Again, he told me, "I will be back in a minute. Get ready before that. There is a stream nearby. You can bathe there". Saying that, he went away without noticing my face. I wept for a long time, alone ~ whom aloneness alone was the soul's company."

"After some time, he entered again with a woman. Pointing to her, he told me, "This is Nachiamma, a prostitute – woman of pleasure. She will teach you something"

"I just retorted without any formality ""For what? I have no experience with prostitution. I don't want to learn anything more than you think. So please let her go""

"What? Oh...You have so much courage now. So, you are Jansi Rani or Chambal Rani? Never more...Don't raise your voice again...Don't try to overact...don't try to act as a good wife or '*pathivratha*'. I heard about your elopement with a milksop '*namboori*' and your return home, right? So, obey what I say, right? village concubine.... phhh" he screamed.

"I was confused about my bleak future. I thought my life ended there. He rushed to me and slapped my face. It was rather painful ~ Raghav, really painful. Both of them left the room soon. I wept without any consolation."

I sat there until dead night ~ that is, 02:00 a.m. Meanwhile, he came and sat on the mud threshold, lighting his cigar. I couldn't move or stand up. Without bathing, without eating I sat there. A lot of anxieties haunted me. Innumerable questions about my future haunted me like a ghost. Shall I be entrapped in this forest? It's like a curse of Ahalya, who was transformed into a stone by the Sage Gautama. Like a stone, I sat there like *Ahalya*. Even *Ahalya* was eventually restored to her human form and freed from the curse after *Lord Rama's* feet touched the stone form. I longed for a touch from Govind now. Shall I end my life? But that was not possible there. This giant man sat in front of this home. At any time, he might step into the room and do something nasty to me. That was sure. It might be prolonged for some hours. After that, I would be ruined by him. Surely, he would take everything from me ~ my goodness, ambitions, aspirations, chastity, and all. I was reluctantly waiting for that wild man to commit his crimes upon me. But what could I do? I told my mind, 'Hold on', and prepared to wait for his approach.

"I felt dizzy, and sleepy but soon woke up on hearing a woman's voice outside. I stood up and made for the door, where I found a woman with a child talking with him. The woman was infuriated and scolded him, saying,

"Is your marriage over? Very good. You are much smarter than I thought."

"So, what! See I am not at all serious with your relation. It's only for time's sake. "He said

"Oh...! So, you are cheating me. See, this child is yours. Looking at his face, can you say that this is not yours? Tell me... tell you bastard...the dirty womaniser. You cheated me and you got a better option now." She retorted."

"Stop it...you bitch..." he told and he rushed towards her.

"He slapped her face and tried to slap her again. Then she clasped his hand and slapped his face back. He became furious and pushed her; at once she fell into the nearby barn, which was not far away from the hut. Her child was frightened and he was crying. I approached the child and swooped up the child in my arms"

"He again approached the fallen woman, held her hair forcibly and said, "What do you think of me? You know I sold you for a moderate income. Now I want to sell that woman also. Yes, I am a pimp. What could you do with me? Shall you kill me? or file a complaint against me? Silly girl...that nearby policeman is my friend. I have already sold out this newly wedded bride to him. I took 2000 rupees as advance. What a fair partition! Is fair enough? Don't you find it curious...you tart..."

""No...I won't allow you to do the same with that woman also...bloody shit...your brothel-keeper...what a dirty procurer" She retorted with pain and she spit on his face.

Being infuriated he took a crowbar placed near the wall and hit her on the head again and again. I was frightened. The boy in my arms – it's you – also cried. I shut his eyes with my hand and ran across the yard without looking back. I didn't feel any tiredness that time. It was relentless effort to save, you (the boy) as well as me. Starved for the whole day, I was very tired. But in that situation, I forgot about my exhausted state. Running, running – where, I don't know. It was dark in the middle of the forest. The sound of the animals frightened me and you. How much time I ran, I didn't know. I looked at the watch but couldn't see anything. How long did I run? I didn't know. I was frightened and exhausted. My throat was dry and I couldn't breathe properly. Your weight was a big burden at that time.

"Somehow, I reached a cemetery; at least a shadow of light was seen. I entered straight into the cemetery. There was only one mercury lamp altogether. Its light glared throughout the cemetery. It was a mysterious place and suddenly I felt complete silence there. I went deep into the cemetery and found a spot to rest, holding the baby in my arms. I looked at your face. You were frightened and tired too. I was exhausted with the strange exertion and slowly closed my eyes for a while. I looked back to see if anyone was following us. But I didn't find any trace of that man. I sighed and both of us slept for a while. The place we halted was surrounded by overgrown bushes. It was a good place for our hideout."

"I don't know how much time I slept there. When I opened my eyes, I found that both of us were in a room. You were still sleeping. It was a closed room. The ceiling fan was rotating at full speed. At first, I was quite afraid. I rushed to the door and knocked for a long time. Finally, I heard the movement of the latch key from outside. A middle-aged woman wearing a large bindi opened the door for me. She was accompanied by a group of girls. All had their faces made up with a lot of cosmetics. I was facing for the first time such a group of women wearing specially ornated lipstick and cosmetics. The middle-aged woman approached me and asked me, "*Are yaar*, who are you? Why are you alone in the graveyard at this odd hour with your baby boy? What's wrong with you ~ quarrelled with your husband and eloped from home?""

"I cried in front of them without saying a word. I was sobbing and weeping but couldn't utter a word. At last, I asked "I need some water. Please ~ it's a request"

"One of the girls from the group went into the kitchen and brought a large bronze pot full of water. I drank it within seconds and asked "If you don't mind, "please, I'm desperate for more water....I beg you""

They again brought a full steel flask of water and gave it to me. I drank that too. You were still sleeping. Your sleeping face aroused their pity. The head woman wearing that large bindi was known as "*Kenjamma*". She asked me "Who are you, my child? Where are you coming from along with this boy?"

"Both of us are coming from a dangerous situation. I don't know how I can explain things. One thing is sure: I want to escape from this place to Kerala. Can you help me, please?"" I told her.

"Everyone out of this room", *Kenjamma* ordered."

"The girls immediately vacated the room."

"Now, actually what happened to you? Tell me everything about you and this baby boy. From where you are coming? How did both of you reach this brothel?" *Kenjamma* asked."

When I heard the word 'brothel', I was very afraid. I have read a lot of stories about brothels in the works of many fictions in Indian Writing in English – in the works of Kamala Das. In those days I thought there were only two brothels in India – one in Mumbai and the other in Kolkata. But in Mangalore I had reached a brothel and I was quite afraid. I said with fear "Madam, I am from Kerala. This place is not known to me. I came here out of sheer fate. I reached these Mangalore outskirts with a man called Bhaskar as a newly wedded wife. He cheated me. This boy is not mine."

"Who? That Bhaskar the rascal...he is a pimp. Is he married? Oh! God...he is a scoundrel. He is a regular customer here. It's his usual business to cheat girls and bring them here and forcefully keep them here as inmates" she abruptly said. She again asked "It seems that you are educated and cultured; and how did you come into his trap?"

"I narrated the whole story ~ from Govind to Bhaskar, the marriage, and also about *Acchan's* predicament and everything connected with him ~ to *Kenjamma*."

"Oh! God! What an embarrassment! But anyhow you are a woman of goodness. At least you saved this boy also, who is not your own. I am proud of you. You are a person with humanity. May God bless you always. But anyhow you have to escape from this place too, at the earliest. Otherwise, you will be entrapped here as a prostitute because this place is not good, dear. We are entrapped here years ago. We had no options at that time. Fate would have it so. Girls here have their own stories. Mostly all the girls came here by being cheated in the form of some love story or a false marriage. Don't you ever think anyone in this world is ready to accept this prostitution willingly? Never, that is my answer. But we did. Why? We don't know. I was kidnapped at the age of twelve and came here. Actually, my native place is in Bengal. From that age onwards I did this job. What to do? No way... Sometimes I think about suicide. But that is one of the vicious sins in Hindu mythology. But children are my weakness. When I saw this boy's face, I felt pity and humanity. This boy must have done something good in his previous birth; that's why he reached your hands. Sometimes I dream about a family – a good husband with two or three children. I long for a baby boy. Sometimes I dream of being with my family, going out for a movie, celebrating occasions like Diwali, searching for a job day by day, finally wishing to land a good job that actually satisfies my needs. I would look after my family. But all are in vain. I reached this dirty place, doing the work again and again monotonous like a machine ~ giving pleasure to each customer physically. Some men torture us. Some others humiliate us. We are the receivers of love, lust and pain. They express their grudge, frustrations and disappointments to us. But again, and again we are falling into this quagmire day by day. The intensity of pain is increasing day by day, dear. What to do? Everything must have been predestined by God. It's the cosmic irony. We can't blame anyone. Anyhow, you along with this boy should be saved. At least before my death I should get some relief by thinking that one person was saved by me ~ "Tears kept falling from her eyes."

Amma too cried when she made a brief pause and said.

"Raghav, at that time I saw a goddess in her. *Kenjamma* – goddess of love and compassion"

"*Amma*, how was my mom looking? Is she beautiful like you? How was she looking? Was she wearing a saree like you?" I asked curiously.

"Your *Amma* was quite more beautiful than me. She was wearing a saree that day, a garden silk – white with blue border. She looked very simple. Your eyes are like your mother's. Even at night I sometimes see her in my dreams – her frightened face, dying face and bleeding cries. But nowadays I see her calm and pleasing face. Sometimes I see her holding my hands and smiling, saying thank you..." *Amma* told.

"And how could we reach our Thrissur?" I asked.

"Yeah, after that *Kenjamma* woke you up and ordered me to come with her. We set out of that old ruined building by a bullock cart. After that by an auto. Then followed a journey by bus. As we alighted from the bus, *Kenjamma* led us to a cozy restaurant, where she insisted on treating us to a hearty meal, her generosity and warmth putting us at ease. From the restaurant, we set off on foot towards Kankanadi railway station, the gentle stroll a pleasant respite before our onward journey. *Kenjamma* took one sleeper ticket from the counter and gave it to me. She also gave me two 50/- notes for travelling expenses. She bought 2 bottles of water for us. After half an hour the train came. She got into the train along with us and made our seats comfortable. We were seated there and she got down. She stood at the window outside of the train. I clasped her hands and touched them with my eyes and said thank you. Then I removed one of the bangles from my left hand and placed it on *Kenjamma's* hand and told her '"Please keep this with you. I don't know how I can show my gratitude to you. You saved two lives. My prayers will always be with you till my death."'

"No, please... I don't need anything. You are a great person. You saved this boy and accepted him as your own child. That's the greatest thing you have ever done in your life. I don't need anything dear. Go for your life dear.... bye...." she said and placed the bangle again into my hands and bid farewell as soon as the train started moving. I watched her, waving my hand till she vanished from my sight. After that both of us alone. You still slept on my lap.

"When I reached Thrissur, my mind was struck with anxiety about how I could tell all these things to my *Acchan*, *Amma* (your *Ammumma*) and others. More than that, the village folk. The newly wedded wife returned within two days; what might be the response of the neighbours? I am very anxious about it. More than that, this boy – obviously this child would be a matter of discourse. How could I tell all those things to my *Acchan* and convince him? I was in a dilemma."

I took an auto up to the village. When I was in the auto my mind became a butt of questions. I couldn't find any answer. When the auto stopped in front of the '*padippura*', *Acchan* was sitting in an arm-chair, reading a book. When he heard the sound of the auto, he anxiously looked at the '*padippura*'. I got down from the auto with the baby boy in my hand and gave the driver the fare. I gave him forty rupees and walked towards the house. *Acchan* stood up and he too walked slowly towards me. He reached me and asked me."

"Why are you coming alone? Baskar hasn't come with you? Who's this child?"

I put the child down and hugged him tightly and cried bitterly. *Acchan* became astounded and patted my hair and said,

'What happened?" he asked"

"I don't know...I don't know. This is my second birth. Your Radha died yesterday. You can see me again out of sheer luck and the deeds done by our ancestors. I want to get inside the room. Please let the boy into our home. I will tell everything in your later life." I told him."

Acchan took the boy in his arms and walked along with me into the threshold. *Amma* came outside and stared at us. When I entered my room along with the boy *Amma* glanced at us.

"I narrated everything I came across within last two days at Mangalore to *Acchan* and *Amma*. They were frightened. Achan's face became pale. *Amma* said "Oh! God! It's really pathetic and haunting. Thank *Krishna*, you saved my child. Hey *Krishna*! Hey *Dwarakadheesh*! Why did you test my child! ". Thus, God ended my marital harmony within three days. It's a cosmic irony. The so-called marital life ended then. But one thing I got from that relationship ~ that is you. You are the sole benefit from that man. Even though you are not my son by blood you are close to my heart, Raghav. *Ammumma* named you Raghav, as the name is a synonym of the name of my *Acchan* – Raman Nair."

"That night, I slept comfortably with you in the same bed. *Amma* slept in the same room. The next day, I woke up very late. I asked *Amma* about *Acchan*. She told me, "Achan left home early in the morning. He asked about you two or three times and instructed you to light lamps this evening at *Sarpakavu*, and then he left."

"I asked, "Where is he going so early *Amma?*"

"Don't know, my child. Before leaving, he touched my hand and only said Why did... I insist that my child marry such a ruthless man? My poor child... This terrible fate is entirely my fault... Take care of Radha and that child..." *Amma* told me.

"That day I was fully thinking about my so-called bleak future. Many questions arose in my mind, but all were unsolved. How could I face my people with this boy? He would be the butt of questions. Anyhow, I made up my mind: first start the tuitions for students as I had done before, and then write the PSC exams. Anyhow, attain a job. That's the only sur name as far as a woman is concerned. I took a bold decision. I along with *Amma* made you bathe and bought two or three new clothes for you. You adjusted with us that day itself, I knew. *Acchan* didn't turn up yet that day. I lit the lamp in the *Sarpakavu* that day. After lighting the lamp, I prayed to the idol of *Vasuki* – the serpentine God – and asked him silently, ""Why did you punish me so ruthlessly? Please help Govind. For my sake, he is suffering now. I beg your pardon. Please don't kill him." "Tears rolled from my eyes, and I wiped them off with the *anchal.* "

"When I entered the veranda, *Amma* asked me, "Your father didn't turn up yet, Radha? Where he has been going in these odd hours? It's becoming dark, and the month of Virgo is going on? It will darken the surroundings at an early hour. The cow is still mewing from the orchards. Please bring that cow from the orchard and tie it in the cowshed. That's a good girl."

"When I crossed the veranda, *Amma* caught my hand and said "My dear child, be a good girl, right? This false marriage shouldn't affect your head. Study well and attain a job, right? We all are with you. Don't worry."

I nodded my head and clasped *Amma's* head and kissed it. Then I walked briskly towards the cow who's tied rope was missing. I searched here and there but it was in vain. I couldn't find the rope. Meanwhile, the cow was mewing continuously, looking at the motor shed, nearby the *Sarpakavu.* When I saw the motor shed, I returned to my memory lane about the day before my wedding night, about Govind, and finally *Acchan's* approach to call me back. I just stared at the motor shed and reluctantly approached it. "Why is this cow mewing without any provocation so many times?" I asked myself. "

"When I opened the door of the motor shed, I was taken a back. I screamed with fear at seeing *Acchan's* hanging body. The rope he had taken was from the cows. I was quite alarmed and screamed again. Soon the neighbours and

Amma came with a thud. All are thunder stuck. I clasped *Acchan's* legs and screamed bitterly, "*Acchaa*...why did you do this? You left me all alone...*Acchaa*...you left me all alone..." "*Amma* felt unconscious at the moment. Thus, again, fate played a pivotal role in my life, Raghav. We three were all alone in the chaotic world – *Amma*, that's your *Ammumma*, You and me – once again left alone."

"I too was frozen like a dead body. I couldn't talk. Words were not coming from my throat. A pain that was so severe. I thought at that time that this period wouldn't pass easily. *Acchan's* smiling face was filling my mind with the contrary image of his hanging body. When I thought about his hanging face – eyes closed, – I immediately woke up from my sleep. I was really going into depression at that time. Months and years passed by. *Acchan's* sad face even today haunts me and my life. That could not be substituted by anyone. It is often said that behind every great daughter is a truly amazing father."

"After the postmortem, *Acchan's* corpse was brought home. Those days can never be recalled. It was my elder brother who performed the last rites. Gradually, everyone left. After the sixteenth day of demise, the elder brother also left for Delhi. We – *Amma*, myself and you – were left alone. I started taking tuitions again. Slowly, I started attending coaching sessions for the PSC exam. Once when I was on the way to the post office, I met Krishnettan who was *Acchan's* friend. He said, "I was actually planning to meet you."

"Is there anything important?" I asked. He continued. "It was I who went to the hospital with your dad's corpse, for autopsy. After the usual procedure, they handed over his belongings. Among the things that I received, I found a letter addressed to you. I had planned to bring it to you several times but I just couldn't. Every day, I would put it in my pocket. Anyway, now that I have seen you, I would like to hand it over. You must read this. Don't worry. *Acchan* will always be with you. We all are there with you, dear. He was my soulmate. You can consider me as your own father, right?" When I received the letter, I was very anxious. I rushed home after taking that letter from Krishnettan. My hand shivered while reading it."

To my daughter,

I was a failure in every sense. It proved to be so in your case as well. I know I'm the one responsible for all that happened in your life. I don't have the guts to face you. I should be born as your father in our next birth.

Pardon me.

The letter concluded with his apology. *Amma* wiped away the tears that had been streaming down her face with the end of her saree.

"So, after a lot of efforts, I managed to get a posting as LD Clerk at Vadakkancherry."

"I still have the letter with me. My dad's letter. And Govind's letter too. In short, I lived these years, with those letters as my close companions. The job came as a blessing, Raghav. It helped me educate you and bring you up."

This sharing made me shudder. I too wept unknowingly. *Amma* continued. "Although we are not related by blood, I am still your mother. A woman need not give birth or breastfeed to become a mother. She can perform all the duties of a mother and be a real mother who is content in life. That's what I am to you, Raghav. Amid this chaos, I continue to live, and you are my destiny."

After the long narration of the story, *Amma* paused. I didn't ask anything more. We silently sat at the *thinna* (small partition wall with sufficient width where people can sit) for a long time. How much time we spent there we didn't know. Then I broke the silence and asked "*Amma*...Its 3 a.m. now. Hardly 6 hours, you have been narrating the story about myself and you. I don't know how I can show my gratitude to you. You gave me your life. For my life, you lost everything. For me, you sacrificed everything, right? Your life, your love life, all your dreams, isn't it? The saddest thing is that you lost your father – that is the most tragic aspect of this fatal drama. So anyhow, I want to make you happy and peaceful in your latter life. That is my word, my dear *Amma* – you are my soul, you are my pole star. You are my goddess, *Durga*."

That's all about *Amma*'s story and the bond between me, *Ammumma* and *Amma*.

My Mother's Wedding

The very next day, I went to Govind's. *Ammumma* had told me about his ancestral home, which is not far from ours. His ancestral home is a *nalukettu* - such a gigantic house. It's the last end of a ring road. I opened the gate, which was unusually large. There was a wide threshold - an open space surrounded by huge *thinna* made of wood.

I pressed the calling bell, and it played *gayatri mantra* inside the closed main door, which I could hear. A woman opened the door for me and asked very politely, "May I know who is this?".

She was wearing a simple *setmundu,* that has a black border. Her bindi is very large - not artificial. May be the *kumkum* from M*ookambika* – the abode of the Goddess universe. She had long hair, put up very neatly like my *Amma.* She wore a leaf of *thulasi* in her hair. No cosmetics on her face. At the top of the *kumkum* there was a small mark of sandal wood paste. Like *Amma* she spoke very politely. Her eyes had a sad expression. They betrayed her melancholic mood – the same I had, seen in my *Amma's* eyes. She smiled and asked, "Excuse me, may I know your name, please...?".

Even her smile was radiant, like a cascade of light illuminating everything around her.

I replied softly, "Actually I want to see Govind sir".

"Govind mama has gone outside. He will be back within a minute. You can sit here." She wiped off the dust on a nearby wooden chair, and asked again,

"Would you like something to drink – tea, coffee, or buttermilk?"

"Anything...no choice at all," I told.

While I was sitting and reading a newspaper, Govind Sir entered the threshold and said "Are you not Raghav? don't you?"

I was quite surprised to hear that question ~ really quite surprised. I had heard *Amma's* words a lot about this Govind, but this was my first time seeing him. Then he truly surprised me.

"How can you identify that I am Raghav?" I asked, smiling.

"I had an intuition that if someone came looking for me at home, it would have been you, Raghav – my Radha's son, right? Everything is clear now," he said earnestly.

I stood up and approached him.

"Sit please..." he requested me.

"How's your mom – my Radha and her *Amma*. Is everything okay with *Amma's* health? That is your *Ammumma*" he asked again.

I was quite surprised again; all the things at my home were known to him clearly.

As I continued talking with Govind, the woman who had opened the door for me came over with a bronze glass of butter milk. She carried it with the end of her saree wrapped around the bottom of the glass - just like *Amma* and *Ammumma* did. After serving me the buttermilk, she went back inside. I took a sip; it was absolutely delightful. The flavours of curry leaves and green chilies were incredible. I asked Govind directly, "Sir, who's this woman? You haven't married. Your siblings, right?"

"No, Raghav, she is my niece. She works in a nearby aided school as a Lower Primary teacher. Actually, after my mother's death, I felt isolated and lonely. From childhood onwards she has been with me. Her parents died in an accident while she was studying in eighth standard. After that, her only guardian was me. Again, fate haunted her in the form of a divorce - like Radha. That man was a sadist. She struggled a lot and adjusted for a long year. When she got a job, she left him. She has a daughter too. She is studying in a nearby school in the ninth standard. Actually, they are my sole family now" Govind said in a monologue.

I felt a pang when I heard the whole story of that woman. Why had God punished such innocent and poor people like this? "What's her name?" I asked again

"Bhumi, and her child is named Adhiti," Govind said.

"Then...what else, Raghav? What are you doing now? I heard that you are in Bangalore for a job, right? And how's your job going on? I hope everything is good with you – and what is your purpose for this visit." Govind asked abruptly

"No...nothing special," I said.

"Hope you are searching for a partner, right? It's high time to get married because you are 30 or 32 now, right?" Govind asked.

"No...not now. I have some plans. I quit the job in Bangalore. I want to stay here because *Ammumma* is aged. I want to make my *Amma's* life more comfortable. I have written a lot number of tests. I hope one of those may crack." I continued, "Are you single now, Govind sir? Are you feeling bored? This lone life?" I asked.

"Yeah, sometimes life is like that. It plays queer tricks on a man. I feel emptiness now because my mother died last year. Waiting for someone – hoping against hope – is a pleasure, dear. I couldn't accept anyone except Radha – your mom – in my life. I am 61 now. You mother retired from service last year. She would be 56 now," Govind said and continued

"Actually, I thought you were coming here to invite me to your marriage. I am happy to hear that news because after your marriage Radha may come with me. It's my false dream, no idea. But hoping against hope is my dream nowadays."

My face filled with gratitude and pleasant. I told him "My mother still loves you deeply, sir – more than anything in the world. My life is a testament to her devotion. Would you consider marrying my mother, who has preserved her purity and innocence?"

"Why not? I have already given all this life to her very early dear. I fully accept her as my wife. If you and *Ammumma* are willing. I 'll cherish and care for my Radha till my last breath, treasure her like a precious diamond. I'll protect her with the same fierce devotion as a serpent guards its most valuable gem." He approached me, took my hands in his, and pressed them to his forehead, breaking down in tears like a child. I was overwhelmed too, and we both wept together.

After our initial conversation, I asked Govind sir if he intended to marry my mother. He wholeheartedly agreed. Then, I returned home and shared my plan with *Ammumma.* She too was completely in favour of the idea and said, "She cried through an entire lifetime; now it's time for her to smile forever. Tell Govind to finalize the wedding date – I will take care of everything."

Ammumma's bold decision truly impressed me. I had been making many plans for my mother's wedding, and amidst all these preparations, I received an appointment memo from the Government of Kerala. It felt like a blessing because, just as I was beginning to think about marriage, I also secured a government job. This gave me a sense of security, knowing that my livelihood was assured for the next few years.

I wrote a poem about my mother's wedding at night in my diary. I decided to invite everyone in person, by going to their homes and speaking to them directly—not through phone calls, WhatsApp messages, or scanned PDF invitations. I was really excited about my mom's wedding and kept imagining how beautiful she would look in her bridal dress. I was still full of excitement. Here's how my poem turned out:

My Mom's Wedding

Yes, my mother's wedding blooms this Wednesday night,
The sacred pudava exchanged between morning's light—
From nine till ten, the hour set in gentle grace,
A simple hall nearby, adorned for this embrace.

My heart is full, a joy I cannot hide,
To stand beside her on this cherished tide.
A hundred guests shall share the festive cheer,
Relatives, friends—all those we hold near.

For her, a gold chain—two pavans in gleam—
Yet far too small for her love's endless stream.
Her sacrifice, her strength, her quiet art—
No jewel could measure the depths of her heart.

My mom's wedding was going to take place on Wednesday. The *pudava* ceremony would be held between 9:00 a.m. and 10:00 a.m. I booked a small community hall near our village for this special occasion. I felt very happy to be a part of my mom's wedding. After the ceremony, I planned a lunch for about 100 people and invited close relatives and friends. I also bought a 2-pavan gold chain for my mom. Though it's a small gift compared to all the love and sacrifices she has made for me, I hoped this wedding will bring her lots of joy and happiness. That's what mattered the most to me.

I asked my mother, Radhamma, about the wedding and the detailed plans. Her face turned red, like the orange sky at sunset. She smiled in a special way. It was a smile full of joy for *Ammumma*. She said, "Oh! Now I'm ready for a peaceful death. All these years, I longed to see my daughter's smiling face. Now I've seen it."

"I have arranged a beautician for a clean and simple make up for the wedding day to come. Are you ready my gracious madam?" I asked mockingly

"*Poda chekka*... you naughty little devil..." Radhamma scolded playfully. Then she slowly came closer and whispered, "At this age, is it for my skin? People might laugh at me... But still, I want to dress up a little, right?" Saying that, she covered her face with both hands and chuckled softly.

"Radhamma, what might be the colour for your wedding saree? Your favourite colour is yellow, right? The colour of Lord Krishna. Shall I buy a wedding saree in yellow?" I asked.

"Yes, yes... yellow...but slightly a modified form. The yellow of mangoes and with a violet border too. Is it available in the textiles shop, dear?" *Amma* asked curiously.

"Of course... why not?" I replied abruptly

I ordered 10 meters of Jasmine flowers to adorn my mom's hair. I also planned a traditional *kurava* ceremony and arranged for a group of young girls to participate. I was not getting tired of preparing; in fact, the more I prepared the more details I found to finalize – from venues to meals, curries, and even the number of puddings.

I visited *Mookambika* temple to collect the '*kumkum*' given by the Adiga for Govind sir to apply on my mom's forehead during the ceremony. I also offered 2 meters of satin cloth to Goddess Durga as an offering.

I know these gestures are small compared to her sacrifices and dedication. She gave up her own pleasure, love and life for me, and I'm forever grateful.

I visited Govind's place and checked on their wedding preparations. Govind Sir was busy with the arrangements for his first marriage. I finalized the time and venue with him. He bought a 32-gram *thaali* for *Amma* and also got two exquisite Kancheepuram sarees.

I asked *Ammumma*," I bought 16 grams of gold for *Amma*. Should I get more?"

She replied, "No dear, that's enough. I have a collection of ornaments that are meant for her.".

The wedding day dawned quietly, with a soft glow of anticipation in the air. We three woke up early, restless and eager, and set about making the final arrangements. I called Govind sir to wish him good morning and offered my heartfelt blessings. He was genuinely excited to hear from me, his enthusiasm clear through the phone. The *muhurtham*—the auspicious hour for the ceremony—was set between 9 and 10 a.m., so everything had to be meticulously arranged: from ensuring the timely arrival of the bride's car to coordinating the priest and other necessary details.

I found myself making more than ten trips on my Honda Activa, going back and forth for various last-minute errands. The beautician arrived promptly and sat *Amma* before the mirror. She even brought along the traditional *Aranmula kannadi*, a polished mirror believed to reveal the most truthful image, especially significant for a bride adorning herself for the final transformation. Under the beautician's care, *Amma* appeared radiant—more beautiful than I had ever seen her. Better late than never, I thought with a smile. The saree she wore complemented her elegance perfectly, its colours soft yet striking.

Before leaving home, *Amma* sought blessings from our only elder, *Ammumma*. She offered *dakshina*, and as they exchanged this gesture, tears welled up in both their eyes. We then boarded a cab headed toward the community hall near town. I sat beside the talkative driver, whose incessant chatter about his own marital life filled the car with humour and odd advice. According to him, he and his wife were the ideal couple in Kerala—a claim that made us laugh softly.

Ammumma wore a pristine white *setmundu*, and we reached the hall at 8:50 a.m. Govind and his team had arrived earlier and were already preparing for the ceremony. *Amma* seemed nervous, her fingers clutching mine tightly as she whispered, "Raghav, do I look beautiful? Is everything alright? Everyone is staring at me."

"You look absolutely stunning," I assured her with a smile. "There's nothing to worry about. I'll be with you."

The most awaited moment arrived. Govind sir, dressed in a golden-bordered *dhoti*, looked dignified and graceful. Together, holding *Amma's* hand, I slowly walked toward the *mandapam*, the ceremonial platform where the sacred rituals would take place. All eyes followed us as we walked, yet *Amma's* grip on my hand never loosened.

When the time came, Govind handed *Amma* the *pudava*, a traditional garment symbolizing the union. *Amma* touched his feet in reverence, and in return, he tied the sacred *thali* around her neck. The *kurava* girls burst into an extraordinary cry of celebration, filling the air with joy and laughter. In that moment, my mother became a bride.

Words cannot express the gratitude I felt toward *Amma.* I simply wished for her happiness—that she finds peace and contentment in this new chapter of her life.

Soon it was time for *Amma's* departure from her childhood home. Holding a lamp, she stepped into the ceremonial farewell. *Ammumma* and I stood by, tears in our eyes as we bid her goodbye. Just before leaving, *Amma* bent to touch *Ammumma's* feet, and then clasped my hands gently, pressing her lips to them in a silent blessing. Without looking back, she entered the waiting car where Govind, Bhumi, and Adhiti sat ready. The vehicle moved slowly down the highway as *Ammumma* and I waved, tears streaming down our faces.

Thus, Radha found Govind as her husband. But it wasn't merely about love. When the right person enters your life, something far deeper unfolds – a quiet transformation. They don't stir up confusion or bring chaos; instead, they offer a sense of calm and clarity you never knew you needed. They don't dwell on the wounds of your past; they see the strength etched into your scars. With their presence, you feel encouraged to rise again, to heal, and to grow into the person you were always meant to become. It isn't simply a bond between two souls – it is a partnership, a shared journey toward becoming the best versions of yourselves.

The house, once vibrant, felt hollow without *Amma's* presence. After the feast concluded around 2 p.m. and all bills were settled, we returned home. Opening the door, an emptiness engulfed us. Without her, the home felt like a void, a vacuum where laughter and warmth had once resided. *Ammumma* went straight to her bed and lay down in silence, while I sat quietly on the *thinna*–the very spot where *Amma* and I would sit together, sharing stories and tea.

That night, I slept in the room with *Ammumma*. I fetched a mat and a pillow from the cupboard and arranged them on the floor, near her bed, unwilling to be far from her.

Epilogue

As I narrated the whole story, it felt as if I was wiping away years of silence. I stopped, sighed softly, and sat in quiet reflection. Hiba Fathima, my former student and a reporter for a reputed channel, too fell into a thoughtful pause, unable to ask anything further. For a moment, the weight of our long conversation hung between us.

I gently broke the silence, hoping to ease the heaviness that had settled over us. "What about your parents? Are they all doing well?" I asked.

"My father passed away last year," she replied softly. "Now it's just my mother and me at home. My siblings have moved away–some for studies, others for marriage. I'm engaged. My fiancé is a doctor working in an Indian hospital in Dubai."

"That sounds wonderful, dear," I said with genuine warmth. "I'm truly happy for you... from the bottom of my heart."

She smiled, but glanced at the clock. "It's time for me to leave. My train departs at 11:30 p.m. from Kochuveli in Thiruvananthapuram. We've talked so much–I'm really impressed by your story, sir. It's more than a story—it's a sacrifice. You and your mother... you've sacrificed so much. A lifetime of it, right? But anyway, it's time for me to go."

"Let me do this," I offered. "It's late, and I'll accompany you."

She hesitated. "Sir, please don't trouble yourself. It's only 10:30 now..."

"No, dear," I insisted. "It's already late, and the station is a bit far from here. I'll come along and see you off."

Without further protest, I booked a cab, and together we headed toward Veli railway station.

During the journey, Hiba turned to me again and asked softly, "So after your mother's marriage, how did you come to adopt Adhiti as your daughter? And... what's the reason behind it? Only if you don't mind sharing. Trust me—I'm not asking out of curiosity. These thoughts are just in my mind. I'll keep them to myself. You can trust me. Even if I write something for the interview column, I'll only publish your profile. Nothing more."

I smiled gently before responding. "A year or two after that, *Ammumma* fell seriously ill. I took care of her as best as I could. But around that time, I was transferred to a new school. I joined as an LD Clerk at Chavakkad, but later I was promoted—to High School teacher, and eventually to Higher Secondary teacher, as you already know. Because of the transfer, I couldn't be with *Ammumma* as much as I wanted. Later, I was posted as Principal at Kasaragod. I couldn't let go of the opportunity, so I had to leave. I forced myself to go.

"I tried to visit every weekend. Sometimes I even took commuted leave to be with her. During those times, Bhumi and Adhiti would help care for *Ammumma.* Occasionally, *Amma* would also come and assist. So, on the weekends when I returned, Bhumi and Adhiti were always there, supporting me, helping me look after *Ammumma.*

"A year later, her condition worsened, and she passed away. But before she died, she held my hand along with Bhumi's and whispered, 'Before I leave this world, I have a wish. My Raghav is all alone. I cannot go in peace unless I see him married. But the time has come—I must go. At the very least, you must care for him, won't you? I know you love him dearly. Please don't ignore my words. He will be a good partner for you. He will also take care of your child.'

"That was *Ammumma's* final message before she closed her eyes.

"At first, I couldn't accept it. But gradually, I agreed. *Ammumma* was more than family—she was my spiritual guide. So, here we are now, living together as a family in the ancestral home. Radha is destined for Krishna; her purpose in life is to unite with him. Similarly, Raghav is meant for Sita—the goddess of the earth—Bhumi. I believe that is how it was meant to be."

I paused, letting the words settle between us.

By the time we reached the station, it was 11:20. The train stood waiting on the second platform. I took Hiba's luggage and hurried with her through the crowd. After locating the coach, I helped her settle into S4. I bought two bottles of water and some snacks and handed them to her. Just as I finished, the train began to move precisely at 11:31. As the train began to move, she touched my hands and said "Thank you, sir... Thank you very much." I waved goodbye. She waved back. We kept looking at each other until the train disappeared from sight.

As I journeyed back to Rajeesh's place, the landscape of my thoughts began to unfold, revealing the contours of my destiny. In that moment, a profound realization dawned on me: life, in its essence, is a relentless pursuit of problem-solving. It is as if each challenge we overcome paves the way for the next, a perpetual dance with the unknown, orchestrated by the divine. And in this intricate waltz, what we truly acquire is not wealth or accolades, but the wisdom and strength garnered through sacrifice – the true currency of our existence.

The End

Glossary

Amma – Mother

Ammumma – Grand Mother

Kasavu – Border of a dhoti. Golden in colour

Acchan – Father

Varutharacha Sambar – A popular curry in south India made by grinding and frying coconut along with the vegetables

Idlis – a south Indian steamed cake made from a batter of ground rice and lentils. It is usually served with sambar

Lord Padmanabhaswamy temple – It is a historic Hindu Temple located in Thriuvananthapuram, Kerala, dedicated to Lord Vishnu.

Vapachi – means Father in Muslim custom

Yakshagana -- A popular folk-art form in Karnataka

Thozhan – Close friend

Sadhya – A feast served in banana leaves with a lot of dishes along with the pudding

Payasam – Pudding

Kumkum – Red powder for bindi. It's a mixture of red colour usually worn on forehead of a woman.

Pandimelam – It's a classical percussion concert or *melam* led by the ethnic Kerala instrument called the *chenda* and accompanied by *ilathalam, kuzhal* and *kombu.*

Panchavadyam – *Panchavadyam,* literally meaning an orchestra of five instruments, is basically a temple art form that has evolved in Kerala.

Kudamattom – It refers to a ritual during the Thrissur pooram festival in Kerala. It's the spectacular, swift and rhythmic exchange of brightly coloured and sequined parasols by handlers on caparisoned elephants at the Thrissur Pooram festival.

Ilanjithara melam – *Ilanjithara melam* is an assembly of percussion performance artists held at Ilanji tree at the courtyard of the *Vakdakkumnathan* Temple.

Setmundu – A *setmundu* is the traditional two-piece outfit for women in Kerala

Sarpakavu – It means 'the abode of snakes' is a sacred grove of trees near traditional homes in Kerala.

Kavu – the short form of *Sarpakavu*

Mama – Mother's younger brother

Vrata Katha – it is a collection of Hindu fasting stories and rituals.

Padippura – it's a traditional, arched gateway, sometimes without a lockable gate, found in Kerala architecture that serves as an entrance to the main building.

Pathivrutha – It's a Sanskrit term referring to a Hindu concept of wife's conjugal fidelity and devotion to her husband.

Namboori – a Brahmin youth

Dwarakadheesh – ruler of Dwaraka – Krishna

anchal – loose end of the saree (pallu)

Kanaya – alternative name for Lord Krishna

Narayanan – alternative name for Lord Vishnu

Yogeswar – Lord Vishnu

Deeparadhana – It's a key ritual in Kerala temples, performed at dawn and dusk where priests wave lit lamps, such as pyramidal or *nagaphana* lamps in front of the deity. It's a moment for prayers.

Thinna – refers to a porch, veranda, or raised platform in front of a traditional house in south India.

Naalukettu – It's a, traditional, large, single- story mansion from Kerala, India, featuring four blocks arranged around a central, open courtyard designed to house a large joint family under a matrilineal system.

Pudava – A new saree gifted by husband to a woman

Aranmula Kannadi – A type of mirror

Dakshina – a ritual before marriage by giving betel leaves and money

Pavan – A *pavan* in gold is a traditional South Indian unit of weight, especially in Kerala and Tamil Nadu, equal to 8 grams of gold.

Halli – in Kannada means "village".

Poda – an informal remark means "go away"

Chekka – a slang term for a naughty boy

Ahalya – The story of Ahalya appears in the story of "Ramayana". Ahalya wife of sage Gautama, was cursed to turn into a stone after she was tricked by the god Indra. The curse was lifted when Lord Rama, as he was travelling with Vishwamitra, touched the stone with his feet, restoring her to her original form.

Thulasi – (or *Tulsi*) primarily refers to the sacred, aromatic Holy Basil plant revered in Hinduism for its spiritual and medicinal properties.